DANNE

j. a. alba

First Edition

Published by *j. a. alba*
ISBN 979-8-9988040-0-7 (paperback)

Printed in the United States of America

Editorial Note:
This work was edited in part using **Grammarly** and services procured via **Fiverr** to support clarity, grammar, and style during revision, including design, formatting, and editorial consultation. All creative content, voice, and intellectual property remain the sole work of the author.

Image Note:
The images featured in the novel DANNE were generated using MidJourney AI. The author holds the legal rights to use and reproduce these images within the context of this publication.

For permissions, inquiries, and rights, contact:
rights@dannebooks.com

"For the truths that didn't need permission—only room."

TABLE OF CONTENTS

PROLOGUE

"We plan for our sound to go inside the soul of the person, and see if they can awaken some kind of thing in their own mind—because there are so many sleeping people."

—Jimi Hendrix

I can't tell you exactly when I got the idea for a dragon tattoo.

Maybe it was after the fallout with my father.
Maybe after that first panic attack.
Or maybe it was always there—quiet, patient—growing roots under everything else.

At first, I thought it was just a phase—something I would grow out of. Then I thought, maybe I need a mark—on my arm.

I could already feel it—the needle, the sting, the skin tightening—as something permanent tried to remember itself through me. It was my way of releasing all I'd been carrying.

I told only one other person about it. Not because I trusted her, but because the silence had gotten too loud.

Annie had this gravity to her. She didn't wear black. She embodied black. Like gravity—a walking eclipse. If you played

1

"Come As You Are" on a dying jukebox in a blackout, she'd be the one barefoot in the corner, asking if you brought the truth, or just the version of the story you've rehearsed. She made you feel seen without spotlighting the damage.

Some people make you confess. Annie made you say the thing you swore you'd bury forever. With her, broken didn't mean ruined; it meant unfinished.

▲▼

We were walking the pier off Dyckman.
No streetlights. No noise. Just the river, hovering in the dark.
The kind of dark that listens. The kind that remembers.

"Where are we going?" she asked—like she already knew.

"Just trust me," I said. "I'm not gonna try anything."

She smiled, crooked and sharp. "And how do you know I don't want you to?"

The river exhaled—slow, black, steady.

I ran my hand over the inside of my arm where the dragon would go, where it had always belonged.

"This spot," I said. "I've been thinking about it for a while now. A dragon—not roaring or flying. Just sitting. Still. Like it remembers what I did."

She reached out and touched it. Soft. Deliberate. Like she was anchoring something real.

And for one moment—long enough to feel, too short to

name—the air between us shifted.
If either of us had leaned closer, everything might've changed.

But it wasn't the ink I felt. It was the weight behind it.
The smoke I'd breathed. The fire I had started—and hadn't
stopped.

"That's where it belongs," she said. No tease. No smile. Just
knowing.

She looked at me—not with pity, but with clarity.
She saw it—the thing I hadn't said. The shape of the guilt
curled up inside me. Because once you name the dragon, it
doesn't just wake. It turns its head. And it never forgets your
voice.

She didn't speak. She let the silence answer for her. And in that
silence, my mind filled in the rest: the regret, the damage,
the part of me I'd been pretending wasn't there.

When I looked back at her, I didn't see Annie anymore.

I saw the dragon. Wings tucked. Not asleep—just waiting.

CHAPTER ONE

Blessed by the Pope?

Six days before it all cracked wide open, I hit the bodega.

Overhead, the lights bled into the sidewalk. The street wore its neglect plain as day, like nobody had cared for it in years. The city pulsed—muffled, heavy—a low heartbeat trying to outrun its own shadow.

Inside, the smell hit me first—burnt oil, old condiments, and that faint, sour smell lurking in the back of the fridge. The fluorescent lights cast a tired yellow glow, their steady buzz filling the room—the kind of noise that made the quiet feel suspicious.

At the counter, Stanley—self-declared monarch of the bodega—was hacking through a phone call like a man wielding a machete in a word jungle. Disgruntled, Mrs. Garcia had once again summoned divine frustration.

"Sí, Señora, yo puedo entender su frustración."
(Yes, ma'am, I can understand your frustration.)

Stanley sighed, pacing between rows of flaming hot snacks and a shelf that looked ready to start a fight. At one point, his hand drifted toward the bottom shelf where a .38 had lived for years, tucked behind a false panel. No one ever mentioned it. But it was there. Quiet as a prayer Stanley kept forgetting he knew.

Then he dragged the phone away from his ear like it was contagious and muttered, "Bendita seas, Señora," (Blessed be, ma'am)—like he meant the opposite.

Stanley was the kind of dude who claimed his cousin played for the Yankees, and swore two-day-old empanadas had the healing powers of Lourdes holy water. On the counter, a faded photo of his daughter—kindergarten smile under a cracked magnet— sat crooked under a lottery sign.

In the back, Chico was in another dimension constructing what looked like an altar to a forgotten saint of expired goods. Cans. Candles. Coffee tins. Chaos curated into art.

That was Chico. Always had been.

We met over a year ago in Cabrini Park. I was skateboarding— hat tilted somewhere between cool and clueless—and he was hunched on a bench, nose-deep in a book wrapped in a brown paper bag like it was classified.

The dude was a menace with books—two days, tops. He didn't just read. He ingested. Dog-eared, underlined, carried around like kin. Every story carved itself into him.

So naturally, I had to ruin his peace.
"Yo, what page you on?"
"One seventy-seven," he said, tight-lipped, like I'd just asked for his social security number.
"That's a good part."
"Thank you."

I coasted away. Then rolled back.

"Cool hat," he muttered, still reading. "It means 'love' in sign language."

I froze. Flipped the cap around. Squinted at it. "... I knew that. You live in my building."

"Fifth floor."

"Ohhh, fifth floor ... that's where all the pretty boys live, huh?"

"Are you having fun?" he asked.

"You got a girl?"

"That doesn't concern you."

"So that's a no."

"Are you spying on me?"

"No, I'm a professional critic. Like Siskel and Ebert," I declared.

"Siskel and who?"

"Fine. DJ Lobo and Alex Sensation[1] rolled into one."

"And how's that working out for you?"

"Doesn't pay much. Spiritually rewarding, though."

"Can I read my book now?"

"Knock yourself out."

I coasted away. Then rolled back like a roach infestation. Uninvited but persistent.

"Your book's covered."

"Very perceptive."

"Is it a sex book?"

---

1 **DJ Lobo & Alex Sensation:** Two of the most recognizable DJs in Latin urban music. DJ Lobo, a Dominican-American tastemaker, fills late-night airwaves with reggaeton, dembow, and bachata. Alex Sensation, Bogotá-born and New York–raised, bridges radio and club culture. Together, their names signal bass-heavy, bilingual energy.

"..."

"Sci-fi? Illuminati conspiracy?"

"The Brief Wondrous Life of Oscar Wao. Junot Díaz," Chico declared.
Said it like he was announcing a winner at the Latin Grammys.

"Oscar Wao? Oscar Wao! Is that your real personality, or did you rent it from him?"
"It won a Pulitzer."
"Pulitzer? That's like God giving you five stars and a tip."

He didn't laugh.
I didn't stop.

A few minutes later—Rachel. Med student. Jogging shorts.
Effortlessly unbothered.
"Hey, Rach," I waved.
"How's your grandma?" she asked, not slowing down.
"Still crazy. She says hi."

She jogged off. Chico glitched—barely a second, like a record skipping.
"You know her?" he asked.
"Yeah. Grandma used to babysit her."
"That's ... interesting."
"What, like interesting-interesting?"
"She's polite. She's smart. She's—"
"Wait ... are you in love with her?"
"I don't think so."
"Final answer?"
Shrug.
"Ladies and gentlemen! Let the record show: he has perjured

himself in the court of love!" I yelled.

"What?!"

"He lied about his intentions with Rachel!"

"Cut it out!"

"HE'S IN LOVE! HE'S IN LOVE WITH RACHEL!"

"OKAY, OKAY, I'M IN LOVE WITH HER! You happy now?!"

"Relax, bro, I'm just playing."

"Some things are private."

"I get it. She's hot. I'd do her."

"???"

"I mean—I'd do someone like her. Calm down ... I'll talk to my grandma. She'll hook it up."

"Really?"

"Yeah, no big deal."

"Thank you ... Can I meet her tomorrow?"

"Chill. What's the rush?"

"If love is one soul in two bodies, Rachel is my other body."

"Yeah ... no. Terrible idea."

"What's it gonna cost?"

"You can't put a price on love."

"I'll give you Call of Duty: Black Ops II."

"Already got it."

"Fifty bucks?"

"Seventy-five. And I'll throw in her Instagram."

"Deal."

As I skated away, I tossed one final word over my shoulder:

"Fukú."

"That's from the book!"

"I know."

Now, in the bodega, nothing had changed. Only the bench

was the Goya aisle, and the book was a pyramid of sardine cans stacked like a Rosetta Stone only he could translate. Chico didn't erase reality. He bent it. Stretched it like taffy. Turned logic into parable. He wasn't just weird; he was cosmically misaligned, like God hit "shuffle" on his DNA and forgot to press play.

Sometimes when he laughed, it felt delayed—like he had to climb back into his body to find the punchline. And the wild part? He made it feel normal.

But even in his orbit, the illusion cracked sometimes.

SLAM!
Stanley dropped the phone like it insulted his mother. Turned slow, face tight. He exhaled, walked abruptly to Chico.
"This is OUT-RAY-GEOUS, Chico! OUT-RAY-GEOUS! You keep making the same mistake! You keep mix-sing the dog food with the cat food!"

Chico, lost in his head, mouthed Stanley's rage like *Goodfellas* on a loop—every line borrowed, none of it his.
"I'm sorry," Chico said.
"What are you sorry for!? I'M the one who has to deal with da problem!"

Behind him, unseen, I mimed Stanley's rant like I was in the ensemble of Hamilton.
"Mrs. Garcia gets VERY upset when she find out she fed DOG FOOD to her PUSSY!"
"To her pussy," I whispered, letting it hang just long enough for Chico to catch it.

That was it. Anchor dropped. The laugh hit. First Chico. Then me. It rippled through the shelves like an inside joke the

9

bodega was in on.

Stanley froze, authority deflating like a balloon two days after the party.

"Are you LISTENING to me!?"

"Yes, Stanley. I hang on your every syllable," Chico said—stone-faced and noble, like a man reciting Aemilia Bassano[2] on the way to the gallows.

I stepped in.

"Dale, Stanley. Ven, que la vieja quiere algo."

(Come on, Stanley. Let's go, the old lady wants something.)

Stanley stomped to the register, muttering.

Chico didn't move. Still frozen in his silent movie—replaying the moment, still wondering if he'd just won or lost.

"You up for some Call of Duty later?" I asked.

"I'm free on Wednesday," Chico said.

"Bet. But leave the baby shit at home. I'm not your babysitter."

Chico grinned like he'd just found a lost reggaetón track from the '90s.

"Don't let Stanley get to you," I added.

"His wife runs the house. And when he doesn't listen? No chocha."

Chico wheezed—laughter bubbling up like somebody just

---

2 **Aemilia Bassano:** Venetian blood, maybe Jewish, maybe something even darker they didn't dare put in ink. She moved through the court like a ghost in silk—fluent in power, fluent in survival. First woman in England to publish a book of poetry under her own name—and maybe the real voice behind the plays they gave to Shakespeare. That's the part they buried. Took her fire, sold it as prophecy, and gave the credit to a glove-maker's son.

turned his Wi-Fi back on.

At the counter, Stanley gave me a look, like he was waiting for
a joke he hadn't heard yet.
"How's your grandmother?"
"Ahí jodiéndome como siempre."
(Same old—giving me hell, as usual.)

Stanley shook his head, blessing the air.
"She's a very nice lady. Very nice ... Five fifty."
I slid him a five and two quarters.
"If you say so."

I was almost out the door when Stanley called out, reached
under the counter, and pulled up a beige plastic rosary—the
kind that comes in a six-pack.
"Give this to your grandmother. Blessed by the Pope."

I flipped it over: MADE IN CHINA. Looked at the tag.
Looked at Stanley.
"Blessed by the Pope, huh?"
He didn't blink. Just nodded.

I pocketed it anyway. Sometimes the gesture matters more than
the proof.

From the back, Chico was already cracking up. "Blessed by the
Pope?" he mouthed.

Then—a clatter. A can hit the floor.
No big deal. Happens all the time.

Until he bent to pick it up.

When he stood, something shifted—the air felt wrong, like an

11

invisible door had just swung open. His eyes flickered, as if the room had glitched and reloaded.

Whatever he saw, he wanted to unsee.
I'd seen that look once before—right at the edge where sense starts to slip.

CHAPTER TWO

MEDEA[3] with a Chancleta[4]

Treading my way through the dim hallway of my apartment building, a slow, unwelcome shudder crawled up my spine, whispering: you're being watched—like I was a goldfish flailing behind glass. The air felt thick and charged.

I turned, heart pounding, expecting to find the source. But there was nothing there, just the hallway staring back —empty and silent.

But I knew better. In this building, shadows had ears, and secrets didn't stay secret for long.

I paused at my door, hand still on the knob. Another shiver. Sharper this time. This wasn't one of Abuelita's moods. This chill had purpose—deliberate, cold.

---

3 **Medea**: In Greek mythology, Medea is the original ride-or-die—helping Jason steal the Golden Fleece, betraying her family for love, and unleashing legendary vengeance when betrayed. Invoking her here signals scale: Abuelita mirrors that sacred fury, an intergenerational force of justice and pain, wielding both care and destruction—sometimes in the same act.

4 **Chancleta:** Spanish for flip-flop. Casual footwear by design, precision weapon by reputation. Carries the kinetic memory of every abuela who's ever settled an argument without leaving her chair.

The air condensed—not just heavy, but expectant.
Like a shadow leaning in too close.

I exhaled and shook it off, then pushed through the door.

▲▼

My keys clattered onto the mantle, smacking against the miniature plaster Baby Jesus—less a sacred object and more like a mute referee. Above him, St. Michael mid-smite, launching Lucifer into a celestial nosedive.

Still feeling a bit uncomfortable, I retreated to my bedroom— my sanctuary of murmured secrets and cloaked truths.

In my room, there's a photo of a younger version of Abuelita, jaw set like she knew what was coming, holding me on her hip like she was built to carry burdens. No smile. Just certainty.

People talk about matriarchs like myths. But that picture? That's where the myth started. And every time I look at it, I remember: I'm not just her kin. I'm her legacy.

Sprawled on my bed, I dove into *The 48 Laws of Power*,[5] flipping pages while cracking up Diana on the phone with the blow-by-blow of my latest mishap.

"So, I'm in this cab after the Yankees game, right? And the driver? Clearly drunk. Like, 'if I blink too long, we both die' kind of drunk."

---

5 *The 48 Laws of Power*: Robert Greene's handbook for high-functioning manipulators—where emperors, hustlers, and drama queens all get their shine. It's like Sun Tzu had a baby with Niccolò Machiavelli and gave it a TikTok account.

Diana burst out laughing.

"Wait—where were you trying to go?" she asked.

"HOME! I'm just trying to survive, and this guy's driving like it's a NASCAR audition."

BOOM.

The door flew open, and Abuelita stormed in, conducting her own little D-Day invasion—voice slicing the air like a chancla mid-flight.

"Daniel, acústate ... acústate! Mañana te tienes que levantar temprano—para hablar con el doctor."
(Daniel, go to sleep ... go to sleep! You have to get up early tomorrow—to talk to the doctor.)

I sighed, dragging the phone away from my ear.

"Yo no voy pa' allá, eso es pa' gente loca."
(I'm not going there; that's for crazy people.)

"Sorry, Di. Oh right—so I tell the cabbie, 'If you let me out now, I won't report you.' He just goes, 'No, no, I'll take you where you need to go.' Can you believe that?"

Before I could even finish, Abuelita was back on me:

"¡Daniel, te estoy hablando! Tú sabes que esto te viene bien."
(I'm talking to you! You know this is going to help you.)

I inhaled sharply and clenched my jaw.

"Di, I'll call you back. Promise."

Click. Game on.

"¿Por qué me jodes cuando estoy hablando con mi novia?"
(Why are you bothering me when I'm talking to my girlfriend?)

Before she even spoke, I saw The Look—the one that meant my funeral was already planned, and the obituary was going to be short and mean as hell.

"¿Novia? ¿Tú llamas eso una novia? Esa es una cualquiera."
(Girlfriend? You call that a girlfriend? That's just some random girl.)

Then came the death blow. The Latin grandma equivalent of a Mortal Kombat fatality:

"Dios mío, dame paciencia, porque si me das fuerza, lo mato."
(God give me patience, because if you give me strength, I'll kill him.)

But I'd been in this ring before. I knew how to counterpunch.

I flipped the charm switch—full blast. Laid it on thick—like I was pitching a timeshare in heaven. I tried to finesse one of those sacred sleeping pills from her stash.

Nada. She wasn't buying.

This wasn't a negotiation. It was a hostage situation—and I was the one begging for mercy.

"Mira, baboso, ¿quién tú crees que eres? Déjame refrescarte la memoria ... la única que manda aquí soy yo."
(Look, dumbass—who do you think you are? Let me remind you: I'm the one in charge here.)

Her shadow stretched over me. Then came the second blow:

"Y si tengo que darte un par de trompones, te los doy. Tú eres una mierda ... en vez de llamar a tu padre, estás hablando con esa."
(And if I have to give you a couple punches, I will. You're a piece of shit ... instead of calling your father, you're talking to her.)

BAM.

There it was: the estranged father card.
Always on cue. Always landing.

I snapped and called him an asshole. I hated saying it, but it felt like the only thing that'd shut her up.

But Abuelita always won anyway.

She came back harder—like he was the damn Pope.

"Ay, Daniel, tú no sabes nada."
(Oh, Daniel, you know nothing.)

This was followed by one of her TED Talks, and not the funny kind.

"Nadie en este mundo es perfecto. Todos cometemos errores. Y hasta que aprendas a tragar esa amarga pastilla, nunca entenderás lo que es el amor."
(Nobody in this world is perfect. We all make mistakes.
And until you learn to swallow that bitter pill, you'll never understand love.)

I wanted to roll my eyes, but part of me froze.

Not because I hadn't heard it before, but because some sick part of me knew she was right. And I hated that. She'd said it

19

a thousand times. Her mantra—cutting to the core no matter how many times it was repeated.

And it wasn't advice; it was truth—blunt, the kind that roots itself deep and won't let go. And every time she said it, I felt that knot tighten in my chest. A reminder that no matter how far I ran, I'd have to face my own mistakes.

And just like that, the fire died down.
Her voice softened—part lullaby, part final warning:

"Ya, dale, acóstate ya y no joda más."
(Come on now, go to bed and stop messing around.)

I countered with charm at max volume, sweet as syrup:

"Dale, mi amor, un vasito de limonada y una de esas pastillas maravillosas, para que yo pueda dormir ... Tú sí estás linda hoy."
(Come on, my love, a little glass of lemonade and one of those wonderful pills of yours, so I can sleep ... You really look beautiful today.)

But even that wasn't enough and now her patience was beginning to fray. I felt it: I wasn't just negotiating. I was being initiated. Drawn into something older than either of us—a lineage made of sharp tongues and sharper love.

Then—like a miracle—she moved.

Shuffled into the kitchen without a word and started making lemonade.

The cabinet creaked open, and the pill bottle made the unmistakable sound of hitting the counter.

I just sat there, realizing I was just another piece on her board—and that I'd inherited more of her than I ever wanted to admit. I wasn't simply dodging her fury anymore; I was inheriting it. The kind that doesn't burn clean but scorches everything it touches, then dares you to rebuild. I had become part of her myth.

Abuelita isn't just some old lady. She isn't even just my grandmother.

She is Medea—the kind of figure whose wrath, born from deep love, could break anyone who underestimates her.

She is healer, matriarch, spiritual enforcer—part bruja, part war general.

Her tools aren't knives, but chancletas, prayers, guilt, and pills stirred into lemonade. She casts spells the way old women pass down recipes: with precision, fury, and love.

People fear her because she does what men do in battle— but with slippers and scripture.

She isn't wrong. She just tells the truth in a language that burns going down. The pain is part of the package—delivery and message are inseparable.

And I had been underestimating her for years.

CHAPTER THREE

The First Scar

Dawn crept in—nosy, golden-fingered—slipping through the living room blinds, quietly coaxing the day awake.

The alarm clock—a shrill, ungodly menace—tore through the silence, yanking Abuelita out of her dreams like a landlord banging on the door.

Reality snapped into place.
Bare feet slapped linoleum—already in motion before her mind had a chance to argue.

The Ritual:
Eggs, folded till fluffy.
Coffee, black as midnight, bitter as memory.
Bread, kissed by fire—then devoured like prayer.

But the real challenge? Prying my eyes open.

"Daniel, levántate," she commanded—wake up—her voice like a cement block hitting pavement.

I didn't move. Not an inch.
I was one with the mattress, pinned by the gravity of sleep.
A muffled grunt slipped out—half protest, half surrender.

With an eye roll so charged it could shift the atmosphere, she walked off. But deep down, I already knew how this movie ended.

She returned. Armed with a pot of ice-cold water.
And then, she let it rain.

I shot up, gasping like I'd just been born again,
the shock ripping clarity through my bones.

"¡Pero oye! ¿Por qué me despiertas así?"
(Hey! Why'd you wake me up like that?)

I wiped my face, mourning the beautiful, interrupted dream:
me and Halle Berry[6]—right in the sweet spot of possibility.

But Abuelita?
Already back in rhythm.
Humming.
Sipping her coffee.
Unaffected. Unbothered.

Dragging myself to the bathroom, toothbrush in hand, I started crafting escape routes from my doctor's appointment:
Maybe a fever could manifest.
Maybe I could claim an ear infection.
Maybe I could just ... disappear.
Maybe ... I was afraid they'd find something.

Something brewing in the bloodline—a shadow passed down like recipes or rage.

---

6 **Halle Berry**: A famous film actress known for her beauty and facial symmetry. When someone says "Halle Berry," they're conjuring a mood: the crush that stuck, the moment the camera fell in love.

I flopped into a chair, projecting just enough discomfort to seem convincingly ill.

Across the table, Abuelita sat perfectly still—expression carved in thought—as if time itself had paused, waiting for her permission to continue.

▼

When Abuelita was sixteen—fearless and spirited—
she navigated the world on instinct, trusting herself completely.

That's how she found herself slipping out one night, chasing the thrill of Roberto's smile.

Roberto, all devil-grin and easy swagger, was etched into her soul like a Polaroid stuck in time.

"¿Qué tal si nos damos una vuelta?"
(How 'bout if we go for a ride?)

The offer shimmered with temptation.
Yet, a quiet part of her held its breath, unsure why.

She hesitated. Declined. Tried to walk away.
But Roberto didn't take no for an answer.

He flashed a hand signal. From the shadows, two figures appeared.
They grabbed her. Threw her into his car. Resistance dissolved.

There was screaming. Fighting.
But in the end, they were stronger. They took her to a cabin—

remote, buried in the hush between Moca and La Vega.[7] Far from rescue. Far from hope.

There, Roberto's mask fell.

He dragged her toward the stained mattress.
Silenced her.
Overpowered her.
Took what wasn't his to take.

Left pieces of her scattered in that room—ashes no wind would carry.

And Abuelita?
She later told the story like it was a footnote.
Something small. Distant.

But I knew better.

That night wasn't just her scar.
It was the first wound in a story that never stopped bleeding—through her, into me.

I used to think her silence was just silence.
Now I see it's where the pain went to hide.

Every laugh. Every hard stare.
Every burnt piece of toast—armor.

And I was living inside it—sheltered by scars I didn't earn.

▲

---

7 *Moca and La Vega:* Tucked-away corners of the Dominican Republic— where the land grows coffee, the trees whisper secrets, and silence stretches for miles. Farmland. Fog. No neighbors close enough to hear a scream.

Snapping out of my drift, I tried my luck with a half-smirk.

"Abue ... I'm running late. You think you could spot me some cab fare?"

Her eyes sparkled like I'd asked for a million bucks—and a pet tiger:

"¡Ah-ha, pero tú te crees que yo soy rica!"
(Ohhh, so you think I'm rich!)

She said it so smooth, it stung—like a slap wrapped in silk.

I opened my mouth to argue—
but the look she shot me shut it right back up.

I sighed. Resigned to my fate. Guess I was taking the bus.

Abuelita?
She'd walked to work in the rain for years.
I could survive the MTA.

But some mornings, I woke up feeling bruises I never got—
like her pain had climbed into my bones while I slept and stayed there.

CHAPTER FOUR

The Catcher Confession

So there I was—feet floating down a coffin-thin hallway like I was walking the last mile to my own execution.

The door to Dr. Coen's office was slightly ajar. Like a mouth waiting to drink me whole—or whisper secrets to the right thief.

I nudged it open. Walked in like I owned the place. Because frankly I already did. I had mapped it all out in my head: layout, habits, system lag.

People leave breadcrumbs, but I don't follow trails.
I write them.

The detective in me kicked in. I yanked open the cabinet—books and files lined up like foot soldiers.

Then I opened the armoire—bingo. A neat stack of button-downs, a few ties looped like limp linguine.

I straightened the crooked painting—restored balance to the Force.

And there it was: a brass gong tucked behind a potted plant, quiet as a classroom of kids at 11:59—one minute from recess, one spark from chaos.

Obviously, I hit the gong.

The deep hum shot through my bones—jolting me like a defibrillator to the chest.

Meanwhile, behind the office, Coen scrubbed his hands in the bathroom, slow and mechanical, like he could wash the weather off his skin.

Each rinse looked less like cleaning, more like prayer. Resetting before the next soul stumbled through his door.

Then—*GONG.*

He froze, hands dripping, staring like the gong had yanked him from a dream. He shook, adjusted his glasses, and marched back into reality.

By the time he came in, I was already engaged to the sofa— a massive Tibetan book sprawled across my lap like a velvet-weighted oath.
Its pages? A carnival of mandalas, gods, and divine freakiness.

I murmured, "Ouuu, I need her number ... and possibly a chiropractor."

Coen stopped dead, caught like Bigfoot binge-watching Netflix. His eyebrows climbed. Mouth twitched.

Ese tipo? (That guy?) Walks like he already knows the ending. No speeches. No ego. Just the guy who doesn't flinch when the room's on fire.

But here's the thing: he's drunk on his own wisdom.

Believes his truth so hard, he forgets he ain't the only one holding a map.

Doesn't realize the map isn't the territory—until someone redraws it.

And that's where I come in.

"Daniel Almonte?" he asked, half skeptical, half amused.
"Yeah, that's what the Feds call me. You writing a book?"

"I'm sorry I'm late," he said, brushing past the chaos like it was ambiance. "Kindly remove your feet."

I dropped into the chair like the fall was always part of the plan.
He kept jotting notes like the paper was keeping secrets.

Probably didn't know his laptop was held together by expired firewalls and a prayer.

I wondered if he knew what I could do with his calendar,
his mortgage docs, that meditation app he bookmarked like enlightenment came in ten-minute sessions.

He didn't.

Most grown-ups don't. They hear the poetry, miss the panic.
Think it's just a game.

But panic is the poetry. And me?
I don't write poems. I strike matches.

Then I saw it—a figurine on his desk. Horse and carriage.
My fingers were on it before I could stop myself.

Coen didn't flinch. Just placed a hand over it, referee-style.

Time out.

"Do you know why you're here?" he asked.
"Yeah. 'Cause I flashed the family jewels in class."
"No, seriously."
"I dunno. You tell me."
"Tell you what?"
"Why I can't keep it in my pants? Maybe you should sedate
me."

He flipped through my file like it owed him answers.

Didn't realize half that crap was floating on the school's shared
drive.
I'd skimmed it last week during Computer Science. While the
class built calculators, I was poking around admin folders like I
had a lease.

The file read like a bad Yelp review: "disruptive,"
"inappropriate," "likely to influence others."

Yeah. No shit.

He stared. Measured.
Hand still resting on the horse and carriage.

"You went to Holy Cross Middle. Why not Catholic high
school?"
"My mom didn't have the dough. Why, you offering?"

He raised an eyebrow.
"Can we focus?"

"Fine. English class. *Catcher in the Rye*."
"And?"

30

"I said Holden Caulfield's gay."
"Explain."

"In relationships, you got the pitcher and the catcher. Holden's the catcher."

Coen leaned back like I had solved a Rubik's Cube with my teeth.

"And your teacher's reaction?"
"Lost her damn mind. Called me politically incorrect. So I called her a fucking phony.[8] And that's why we're in this ... cunt-nundrum."
"Conundrum," he corrected.
"Nah. Cunt-nundrum."

He almost smiled. Mask slipped.

"Tell me about your father."

Boom.

"My father? Ralph Kramden from *The Honeymooners*—except when he did the *BANG ZOOM*, my mom actually went to the moon."[9]

"And how did that make you feel?"

---

8 **Phony (Holden Caulfield's insult):** The term comes directly from *The Catcher in the Rye*. Holden uses it to describe people he sees as fake. Danne mimics this, both as homage and rebellion.

9 **Ralph Kramden from *The Honeymooners*:** A 1950s TV character known for threatening his wife with *"BANG ZOOM"*—an outdated and now deeply problematic comedic portrayal of domestic abuse masked as humor. The reference darkens Danne's comparison, anchoring his father's violence in cultural memory.

"I was fine. My mom?
Serious black eye. You're eleven. Watching the Yankees.
Parents arguing—some dumb shit about going to Staten
Island.
Mom says no. Dad makes her say yes—the only way he knows
how. Bada bing, bada boom—Jeter hits a walk-off, and my
mom gets a black eye."

I smiled.

"Fucking Jeter. Man's got everything. Babes. The looks. The
watch. God, I wish I had that watch. You think Jeter's good-
looking?" I asked.
"You could say that."

"C'mon, man-to-man. You ever play catcher yourself?"
"Listen—"
"You said Jeter was attractive."
"No, you said that. I agreed."
"So you agree that you're a homo."
"You're deflecting."
"And how does that make you feel?"

Coen went ice cold. Then—a raw, misplaced laugh erupted.

"Danne," he said, catching his breath.
"Yeah?"

"You're funny."

"Tell me something I don't know."

"You're also lying."

The room shifted. Voice low. Steady.

"You know why you're here."
"Bruh—my teacher's soft."

"No, Danne."

Tap-tap-tap.
(He tapped the file.)

"You hacked the school server. Planted a virus. It took seven days to fix."

Silence. Smirk: gone.

"That's dangerous," he continued.

"According to quantum physics,[10] what isn't observed didn't happen."

"I think you're running."

(No wisecrack this time.)

"What if we make a deal?"

"Heard this one before."

"Therapy. No cops. No expulsion. Just me and you."

Soft touch. Hard boundary. Classic redirect.
Almost had me.

"Come here, Doc. Give me a hug."

He hesitated. Hugged me. Stiff. Awkward.

---

10 **Quantum Theory:** A reference to the idea—popularized by the double-slit experiment—that observation (in the sense of measurement) affects physical systems. Danne hijacks this as a rhetorical trick, twisting it into the notion that if no one witnesses the damage, it doesn't exist. It is denial disguised as intellect.

And in that moment?
I swiped his office key. Clean.

"Isn't this ... I dunno ... inappropriate? Hugging a student?"

He jumped like I had tased him.

"Yo, what's that?" I pointed—distraction.

"That?" He softened, voice shifting:

"That's the OM[11] sign.
What was, what is, and what shall be.
Lower curve: dream state.
Upper: waking. Middle: dreamless sleep.
This"—(taps crescent)—
"is Maya, the veil of illusion.
The dot?
Transcendence."

He leaned back, full guru, and breathed in a full Yogic breath.

I squinted.

"Looks like a three, a six, and a backwards nine."

Broke him. He beamed.

"Wow. Never saw that before."

---

11 **The OM symbol (ॐ):** From Hindu and Buddhist traditions, OM
represents the universe's fundamental vibration. Its parts map states of being:
the lower curve is waking (jagrat), the middle is dreaming (svapna), the upper
is deep sleep (sushupti). The crescent is maya—illusion; the dot, turiya—
pure awareness beyond all states. For Dr. Coen, OM isn't just a symbol but a
miniature cosmology, reframing the novel's question: are we awake, or only
dreaming under illusion?

And just as he tried to recover, I lobbed one last grenade:

"You know, Doc, fifty milligrams of Xanax[12] puts you in a very deep sleep."

Boom. Mystic haze: gone.
Zen: snapped. Session: terminated.

"Danne," he said, voice threadbare,
"Our session is over. Please leave."

And who was I to argue?

Some doors you walk into.
Some, you walk out—with the key.

---

12 **Fifty milligrams of Xanax**: A dangerously high and fictionalized dose of a real anti-anxiety medication. Standard medical use is usually 0.25 to 0.5mg per dose. Danne isn't being literal; he's testing boundaries. He's provoking Dr. Coen with the possibility of self-harm, manipulation, or both.

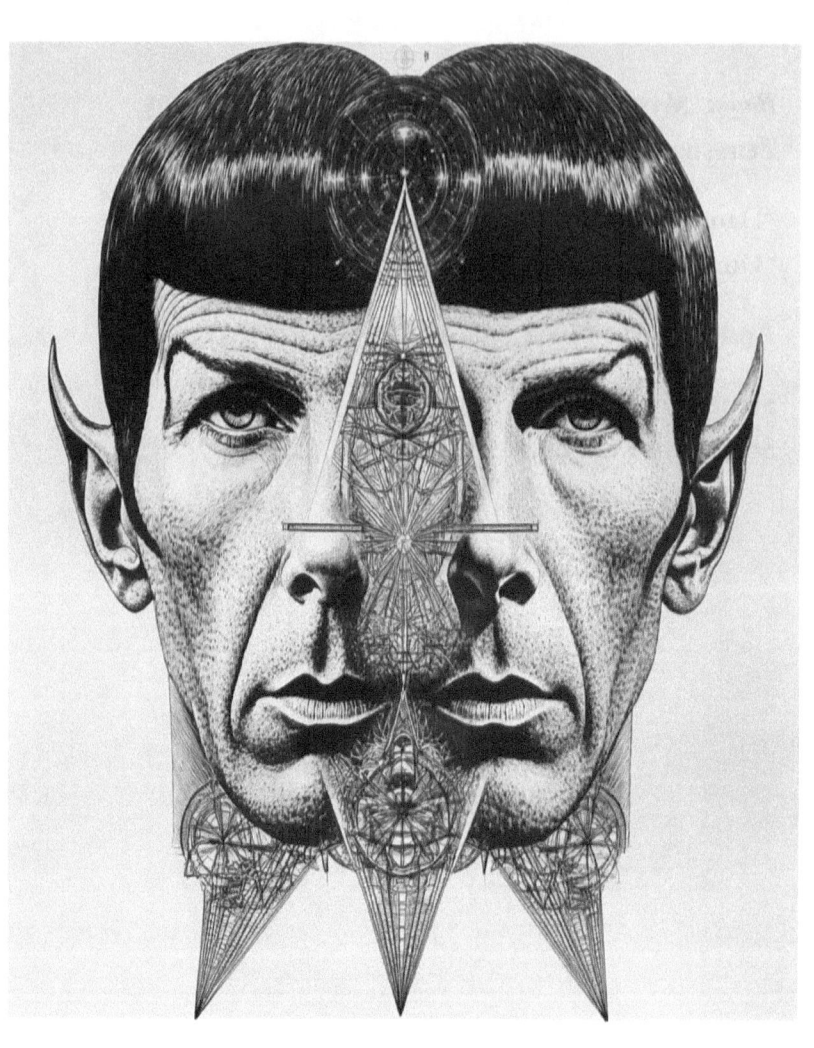

CHAPTER FIVE

I Am Not Spock

Law 33: Discover Each Man's Thumbscrew.[13]
That's what *The 48 Laws of Power* says.
And Diana?
She didn't just find mine; she pressed it like she was born
knowing how.

She's straight outta a Barbie catalog—
if Barbie had a Dominican cousin from Washington Heights[14]
who could cuss you out in two languages
and still make you feel lucky to be the target.

My boys dap me up like I just got drafted—
like I beat the odds and won a prize nobody knew they were
playing for.

---

13 **Law 33: Discover Each Man's Thumbscrew:** A rule from *The 48 Laws of Power* by Robert Greene. This "law" advises finding someone's deepest vulnerability in order to control or manipulate them. Danne's reference isn't just macho posturing; it sets up how Diana disarms him emotionally without force, just precision.

14 **Washington Heights:** A Dominican-heavy neighborhood in upper Manhattan, NYC. It places Diana's identity in a specific cultural context. She's not a generic "hot girl." Her energy, voice, and defiance are shaped by a lived heritage.

Her skin?
Golden.
Like it knows the sun personally.
Like God Himself brushed honey on her shoulders and
whispered,
"Try not to stare too long."
(And you couldn't help but listen.)

Her hair?
A rebellion. Natural—it moves like merengue.[15]
The kind of texture that makes your hands forget what they
were doing.

But those eyes? Ay, Dios mío. (O.M.G.)
Brown. Deep. Enchanted.
Like a riddle with no answer—and you don't want one.
You just want to stay lost.

And that body? Dios Santo.
Her hips? Built for salsa, sin, and rerouting your whole life
plan.
Thighs? Engines.
That ass? A masterpiece—deserves its own exhibit.
Velvet ropes and a line around the block.

Yeah, I could stare all day. And I did.
And still—she lets me. Keeps me there.
One foot in, one foot out. Like she's testing me.
Pulling me in with every smile,
pushing me back when she's had enough.

---

15 **Merengue:** A fast-paced Dominican music and dance genre. When Diana's
hair is compared to merengue, it's not just about beauty; it's about rhythm, joy,
and cultural inheritance. A love letter in metaphor form.

I'll admit it: I'm infatuated.
But it's not just her body.

It's how she knows her worth—without making me forget mine.
She regulates the distance.
Keeps me just close enough to crave more.
It's a game.
A chase.
A feedback loop of flirt and retreat.
And carajo (damn), what a journey.

▲▼

After school—the bell still echoing—I'm walking down Riverside with Diana.
One of those days where the sun's showing off—
throwing gold light around like it's free.
The kind of light that makes you believe people are softer than they really are.

I'm feeling myself.
So, naturally, I reach for that museum-grade culo.
Diana? Too quick.
Swats my hand like she trained with Bruce Lee in a past life.

I lean in for a kiss—she dodges like Mayweather, round twelve.
Now we're dancing.
Suave gato (smooth cat) chasing a ratoncita (little mouse)
who knows how to stay just out of reach—
but not far enough to stop me from trying.

"Diana, there's something different about you today," I say.

"Is it my hair?" she asks, curls bouncing with smug perfection.
"Nah, not the hair. Something about your eyes."
"Oh, my eyes? Qué lindo."
(How sweet.)
"I think you're cross-eyed. Follow my finger."

I hold it up like I'm conducting an invisible orchestra—
then boom, jab it up her nose.
"Dios mío, you're such a pest!"
But her voice doesn't bite.
Tone light. Body loose. Open.

"I'm genuinely concerned," I say. "Something's off. Let me
check again."
Full clown mode. Finger back in motion—
up her nose like I'm digging for treasure.
"Stop!" she groans.

Then—pause.
A flicker in her eyes. A micro-shift.
Like she's waiting for the mask to drop.
Like part of her wants me to quit the bit and just say what
matters.
But I dodge.

"Where'd you get this watch?" I ask, grabbing her wrist like
I'm CSI.

"I bought it," she says. Full sass mode.
"Yeah? Where?"
"At the jewelry store, Sherlock."

"And who was playing Watson?"[16]

She sighs—a classic I'm-not-killing-you-because-I-like-you sigh.
"You're ridiculous," she says, trying to sound mad,
but I see the smile tugging.
"I'm re-dick-u-lous?"
"Yeah. A real dick-u-lous."
"One more round with the magic finger?"
She slaps it away.

And just like that—the air shifts. Laughter fades.
Heartbeat louder. World slower.

Her eyes go thoughtful.
Not mad. Not cold.
Just ... searching.

"Danne," she says, soft now. "Do you even love me?"

I freeze. That cocky grin falters.
Replaced by a weight I can't shake.
This isn't a joke anymore.
But I still try to play it off.

I click on.
"Of course I do, you little fox," I grin.
"I'm the only one who puts up with your shit—
I mean beauty. Your beauty."

"Tell me the truth."
"You want the truth?"

---

16 **"Sherlock"** and **"Watson":** Referencing the iconic detective duo by Sir
Arthur Conan Doyle. Diana's quip calls out Danne's nosy curiosity. His
comeback—"Who was playing Watson?"—is pure jealousy masked as wit.

"Yes."
"Nothing but the truth?"
"For the love of God—yes."

She's fed up.
Wants something real. A break in the pattern.
I grab her wrist. Tilt my head.
Drop into my breaking news anchorman voice:

"I'm here LIVE with Diana, as she shares her innermost secrets
about breast size and facial hair—"
"Can you stop joking for one minute?"

The air tenses. Her breathing's up.
Pupils locked. This is the moment.

And for a second, I feel it—like I'm just a guy wearing a
costume that used to fit.
Like I've been playing this role so long,
I don't remember when it stopped being pretend.

But it's easier to be the comic relief.
Easier to dodge than confess.

So I pull back. Wink at the imaginary audience.

"We'll be right back after these messages."
Then—
"Yes. I love you, you little vixen. Happy now?"

If looks could kill, my autopsy would already be trending on
TikTok.
"Stop or I'll hit you."
"Now we're talking. Can you spank me too? That really turns
me on."

"I'm done."

She spins. Storms off.
But I catch her wrist. Freeze her exit.

In my head: This is the moment I should let her go.
But no—I've got a big mouth.

"Okay, okay—what do you want?"
"Take me on a real date," she says. "Suit and tie."
"Done."
"For real?"
"Absolutely."

She melts.
Lights up like her dress has pockets.
"Oh, Danne. You're kind, you're funny ..."
"You say that to all the boys."
"No. You're a keeper."

"A keeper?"
"You're a forever kind of deal."
"Then how about a little some-sing, some-sing?"

Mood? Killed.
"No way."
"Come on. Just a little—"
"I see what you're doing ... You wanna have sex and pay me off
like I'm some prostitute."
"How dare you?" I say, hand to chest.
"I'm a gentleman. I'd pay you first."

She shakes her head like I'm a song stuck between stations.
"You're impossible, Danne. Same clothes. Same tired jokes.

Grow up—and maybe holla when your game stops playing itself."

Boom—she's gone.
"I was kidding!" I yell.
"Go screw yourself, Danne!"

I grin to myself, muttering,
"I'm gonna have to. You're not giving me any."

But real talk?
I don't want any.
I want her.

And for the first time, I feel it.
She's not bluffing.
She's seen every move.
Read the whole playbook.
And still chose the exit.

That hits different.
Scares me more than I'll ever admit.

Then her voice, floating from the stairs:
"Danne, you know the actor who played Spock?"

"Yeah—Leonard Nimoy."
"He writes *I Am Not Spock*. Swears he ain't the guy.
Then, twenty-five years later—boom—*I Am Spock*.[17]

That's you, Danne.

---

17 *I Am Not Spock / I Am Spock*: Titles of Leonard Nimoy's autobiographies. Diana's use of this metaphor cuts deep: Danne tries to reject emotional attachment but inevitably returns to it. The line reframes his whole arc as a loop of denial.

One foot out, one foot in.
Stuck on a loop.
Déjà vu in reverse."

I pause.
Damn.

She didn't just dodge me.
She decoded me.

I exhale—like she handed me a fortune cookie that needed a
PhD to unpack.
And for once,
I got no comeback.

Just my own voice echoing back—
like I'm stuck in syndication.[18]
Same lines. Same ending. Every time.

Then, from the staircase:
"Beam me up, Scotty!"[19]

And just like that—she vanished.
Left me under the big dumb sky,
replaying the whole thing
like I'd just gone viral ...
for all the wrong reasons.

---

18 **Stuck in syndication:** Refers to TV shows that endlessly rerun. Danne uses
it to describe the pattern of his relationships—predictable, numbing, and on
repeat. It's the chapter's thesis disguised as punchline.

19 **Beam me up, Scotty!:** A catchphrase from Star Trek, used here as Diana's
exit line. Funny, sharp, and self-aware. She leaves with control, turning pop
culture into a mic drop.

CHAPTER SIX

Weight Limits

The city stretched its shadows long and mean, like supermodels stomping down a catwalk—sharp, unbothered, built to intimidate.

And there I was—beat-up sneakers tattooing fresh hieroglyphs into the pavement—when ...

BOOM.

An engine snarled behind me like a pit bull snapping its chain. Some hunk of metal rolled up slow.
It coughed—deep and guttural, like it'd smoked a thousand loosies[20] on the corner.

The passenger window crept down.
And there was Leo.
Grinning like he knew a secret your nervous system already braced for.

"Yo, Danne! Where you goin'?"
His voice had that DJ bounce—like he'd been spinning the

---

20 **Loosies:** Slang for individual cigarettes sold illegally, often in urban neighborhoods. Describing an engine as having "smoked a thousand loosies" anthropomorphizes it—giving it a gritty, street-smart personality.

same set for years but still swore he was killing it.

"Nowhere," I shot back. Cold enough to turn coffee into iced espresso. He flicked his wrist.

"Come on, hop in. We're about to have some fun."

Now, me and Leo? Yeah, we share blood.
But our definitions of fun?
Let's just say, they're mapped on different coordinates.

"Nah, not today. I'm good."
"Don't be a buzzkill, bro. Loosen up," he said—voice dipped in velvet, threaded with command. The kind that bypasses logic and goes straight for the reflex.
"Maybe some other time?"
I started backing away, instincts humming.

Leo wasn't having it.

"Nah, Danne. You're coming—like it or not."

That's the thing about Leo:
He doesn't invite you.
He pulls you in.

Not just a fast-talking hustler—he's a full-blown Diablo in designer sneakers.[21]

Part magician.
Part cult leader.
Part pyramid scheme in human form.

---

21 **Diablo in designer sneakers:** *Diablo* is Spanish for "devil." This metaphor blends religious imagery with street-style swagger. Leo isn't just trouble; he's seductive trouble. The phrase evokes a duality: fear cloaked in charisma.

When his right eye squints?
That's the tell.
LED sign: Bullshit ahead.

You don't get truth from Leo.
You get performance.
A magic trick.
A rollercoaster of half-truths bent sideways.

And when he barks—your nervous system listens before you
do.

"'No' ain't on the menu. Get in the car."

I let out a sigh so dramatic it could've powered a Goodyear
blimp.
Dragged my feet like I was signing up for another episode of
Leo & His Bitch-Ass Sidekick.

Cue the laugh track. Roll the damn credits.

▼

"Danne, this is one of my boys—Corrán,"[22]
Leo said, gesturing like he was pointing out a fire hydrant.

"Corrán. Cool. That's like 'Corey,' but gentrified."

Corrán shot me a look. "What are you, a wise guy?"

---

22 **Corrán:** A rare Irish name derived from *corrán*, meaning "sickle." The
sickle—a curved blade used for cutting grain—becomes the metaphor here.
Corrán's sharp, quick-tongued persona slices through ego and emotion. His
name signals a reckoning. Just as a sickle harvests, *Corrán* trims away pretense,
pushing Danne toward emotional clarity.

"Nah. You just got that Whole Foods look."[23]

Back in the day—before vape shops, café galleries, and ironic mustaches—the Irish ran this city. Brownstones. Pints. Grit. Stubborn pride.

But time?
Time rewrites the code and recasts the players.

In Washington Heights, the lease flipped.
We moved in—Dominicans with soul and swagger.
Turned bodegas into hubs. Made dominoes a second language.
Raised the bachata decibel level 'til the block had a heartbeat.

And then there was Corrán.
A snowflake dipped in salsa.[24]

Skin pale like snow on a minefield—quiet, spotless, and hiding something sharp.
Hair? Auburn inferno.
Freckles? A drunk constellation.
Eyes? Ice-blue, sharp—like he knew where it hurt before you did.
Style? Cultural mixtape. Irish bones, Dominican rhythm stitched in.

---

23 **Whole Foods look:** A nod to the upscale grocery chain tied to organic goods and affluent, urban clientele. Saying someone has it implies they look polished, privileged, even gentrified—out of place in rougher settings. A backhanded jab at Corrán's curated identity.

24 **A snowflake dipped in salsa:** A poetic contradiction. "Snowflake" suggests whiteness or fragility; "salsa" implies Latino heat and rhythm. Together, it highlights Corrán's racial and cultural ambiguity—an Irish-American who moves like he was born in Washington Heights.

Corrán didn't just join the race; he rewired the finish line.

"Where'd you pick this one up?" Corrán asked Leo.

"Family discount," Leo shrugged, like I was a clearance-rack hoodie.

Then—maybe remembering I had emotions—he softened. "What's da matter?"

I rubbed my face like it might smooth out the mess inside my skull.
"Got into it with Diana," I muttered.

Leo scoffed, head-shake full of judgment.
"Forget her. All she does is make you suffer."

Easy for Leo to say.
He loves like a casino—drops chips, walks away.
Me?
I was knee-deep. Not just love. Shame. Silence.
Just a numb ache that refuses to leave.

"Nah, man. She's ... different. She's special."

That's when Corrán laughed.
"There's no special bitch. There's the one you have kids with—and all the other bitches on the side."
He laughed like it was gospel.

But something flinched across his face—real fast, like a memory that didn't ask permission.
Maybe he grew up on that line.
Maybe he learned early: sticking around was optional.

Grin snapped back on. But I caught it—the slip, the flicker, the thing he didn't mean to show.

"You got it all twisted. We've had real moments."

"Bruh, you're hallucinating. Only real moment is when you come," Corrán smirked.

"We'll take you to the park. You'll forget her face," Leo said.

"Mad bitches out there," Corrán added, baiting hard.

"It's not about sex. I love her."

Leo rolled his eyes so hard I heard them click.

"We'll get you on a ride so wild, you'll forget she ever had a name—let alone your number."

I wanted to hit something. Not them—me.
For trying to explain something real to two dudes powered by ego and Monster Energy.[25]

"Yeah, throw his ass on Nitro!"[26] Corrán said—too quick.

Leo's whole vibe shifted.
Like a memory that didn't ask permission.
Just hauled off and hit him.

"Yo, why you gotta bring that ride up?" he snapped.

I perked up.

---

25 **Monster Energy:** A caffeinated drink tied to extreme sports and hyper-masculine culture. Here, it signals volatile, amped-up masculinity—Leo and Corrán running on impulse, not introspection.

26 **Nitro:** A Six Flags rollercoaster used here as a metaphor for public shame. Leo's humiliation isn't just about weight but masculinity and exposure—men strapped into expectations and judged on size, speed, and strength.

"Wait. What's wrong with Nitro?"

"You see?" Leo grimaced.

Corrán grinned like a kid with blackmail.
"Leo had ... an incident."

"Dude, shut the hell up!" Leo snapped—too late.

"C'mon, spill it," I said.

Leo groaned. "A'ight, but this shit ain't funny ...
I waited in that stupid ass line for forty-five minutes. Front row. Prime spot. I sit, pull the harness—thing won't budge.
I suck in my gut, push down—nothing.
I call for help. Two dudes show up, start pushing like I'm a damn couch stuck in a hallway.
One of 'em grunts—'Argh.'"

I was already losing it.

"Then the dude on the speaker goes, 'Is he good?'
And the guy next to me gives the slowest, coldest thumbs-down I've ever seen."

(Leo mimed it. It was brutal. Biblical.)

"How do you put King Kong on a roller coaster?" Corrán howled.

"That's messed up," I wheezed, tears forming.

"One of those dudes definitely copped a titty," Corrán added.

Leo shook his head. "Whatever, man. I'm losing the weight.
Dropped five pounds already."

"Does it count if it came out your ass?" Corrán snorted.

Leo grumbled—but a smirk slid in.

Then came the silence. Thick. Heavy. The kind that settles like bad takeout in your chest.

"Where we going?" I asked.

"To Jersey," Corrán said, gripping the wheel like it was the only thing in his life that didn't walk away.

"Gas is cheaper."

"That's my boy," Leo said, clapping his shoulder. "The cheaper, the better."

"Those damn Sunnis,"[27] Corrán muttered,
like he had Fox News for blood.

I shifted.
"That's lazy, man.
You don't even know who they are."

Leo hit me with the shut-the-fuck-up-before-you-make-me-think glare.
"What's that supposed to mean?"

"You don't even know who these people are."

"Yeah I do. They're the kind that don't shave," Corrán said.

"Fine," I sighed. "I'll shut up."

———————————

27 **Sunni:** One of the two major sects of Islam. Corrán's ignorant quip highlights casual racism—bigotry that hides behind economic or political "concerns." It reveals more about Corrán's upbringing and worldview than he realizes.

"Good," Corrán grinned. "'Cause you don't know what the hell you're talking about."

"Oh, I don't? But you're the genius?"

"Damn right."

"Let's run the numbers, genius.
You drove across state lines to save forty cents a gallon—call it three bucks.
Toll's thirteen. So congratulations: you spent ten extra to feel economical."
I let that marinate.
"They should name an economics class after you."

Corrán turned red.

My words came out too sharp—like I hit something I didn't mean to.
The air changed. Tight. Not hot, just tense.

Then—*SLAM*. The brakes hit.
We lurched like crash dummies.

"Get the fuck out."

"You serious?"

"Does this look like I'm joking? Get outta my car!"

Leo just sat there, taking it in like he kinda liked it.

I shoved the door open. Gravel cracked under my sneakers.
Corrán peeled off like the road owed him money.

▲

And there I was.

Just me, the George Washington Bridge,[28] and a full-blown symphony of honking horns and furious pigeons auditioning for *Birds Gone Wild*.[29]

First time all day my jaw wasn't locked like a bank vault. Something behind my ribs finally exhaled.

The city ahead pulsed like a dare.
Like it was saying, "Come on, genius. Let's see what you got."

And maybe ... maybe I was just dumb enough to take the bait—but smart enough not to choke on it this time.

I started walking. Each step syncing with something real and quiet inside.
Like I'd finally found my own rhythm again.

No masks. No clown routine.
Just breath. Just grit.
Just me—on the long, loud march toward whatever the hell came next.

And looking back? Getting tossed from that car?
Best thing that happened to me all day.

---

28 **George Washington Bridge:** A defining structure linking Manhattan to New Jersey. It becomes a metaphor for threshold—a literal and emotional crossing. When Danne walks it alone, it signals personal transition: from codependence to self-possession, from ego to growth.

29 ***Birds Gone Wild:*** A tongue-in-cheek riff on the notorious *Girls Gone Wild* franchise—infamous for chaotic, over-the-top behavior caught on camera. Reframing it with pigeons adds absurdist humor while also critiquing the everyday madness of urban life. The phrase turns a mundane moment into comic theater, amplifying the chaos of Danne's emotional release.

CHAPTER SEVEN

Better a Punch Than a Bullet

I was back at my crib.
Night thick as motor oil.
The city humming low and mean outside—like a drunk uncle
pacing the stoop, looking for a fight or a story. Maybe both.

I squared off with the apartment door—
that finicky little bitch never made things easy.

Fumbling the key like a drunk threading a needle,
I muttered curses only the lock and God could hear.

Then—*click*. She gave in.

I pushed into the abyss.

The dark didn't just swallow me.
It chewed. Slow.
Wanted me to feel it in the bones.

My fingers swept the wall like a blind pianist searching for a
lost note—until *snap!*—light spilled into the room.

And there she was.
Abuelita.

Dead-center.

Looking like she crawled out of a Dalí painting[30]—robe twisted, hair wild, eyes lit like a busted neon sign that still means business.

Clutched in her hand? A plastic baseball bat.
In that moment, it might as well have been Thor's hammer.[31]

I grinned—pure reflex. Dumb. Guilty.

WRONG MOVE.

WHACK.

She swung like she was resetting my whole spirit.

When the levee breaks, you don't pray.
You don't talk. You listen.

Because every thwack—every righteous, rhythmic beatdown—came preloaded with meaning deeper than any lecture.

"¡Mira, muchacho del diablo!"
(Look here, you little devil!)

"¡¿Cuántas veces te voy a decir que me llames cuando vas a llegar tarde?! ¿Dónde estabas y con quién?"
(How many times do I have to tell you—call me when you're going to be late! Where were you and with who?)

---

30 **Dalí painting:** Refers to surrealist artist Salvador Dalí, known for bizarre, dreamlike imagery. Abuelita isn't just disheveled; she's mythic. The comparison signals her presence as uncanny, larger-than-life, and emotionally unpredictable.

31 **Thor's hammer:** In Norse mythology (and Marvel comics), Mjölnir is a weapon only the worthy can wield. The plastic bat becomes symbolic. In her hand, even a toy carries mythic weight. She doesn't just discipline; she enforces moral gravity.

I shrank instantly.

Voice all bodega-thief guilty.
"Estaba con Leo ... "
(I was with Leo ...)

WROOONGER ANSWER.
WHACK! WHACK! WHACK!

Each hit an encrypted message.
Choose better.
Think smarter.
Feel that, sucker.

She wasn't just mad.
She was the test.
The locked door you don't get through unless you survive the lesson.

▼

And just like that, there he was again—
Leo grinned, bolt cutters loose in his grip—
like a joke and a threat wrapped in one slow swing.

"Go on," he said. "You got this."

The lot behind the fence was blackout—
busted glass, rusted skeletons.

The kind of place that eats flashlights and buries secrets in hubcaps.

"What?" he smirked. "You scared?"

I ducked through first.
Heart pounding like it was trying to file an escape request.
Hands sweating like they knew something I didn't.

The metal scraped my back on the way in.
Felt like the city itself was trying to tell me nah, kid.

And there it was:
A busted-out cop car, sitting in the dark like it had been
waiting just for us.
Like it remembered every chase.

I pulled out the Sharpie. Tagged the hood.
Some half-formed graffiti—barely a name, barely a shape.

Just enough to say: I was here.

Sirens pulsed in the distance—
not close, not far.
Just enough to feel like a dare wrapped in a warning.

Leo hit the pavement laughing before his feet even landed.
The dude bounced off chaos like it was a trampoline.

"If they catch us," he said, "just cry.
They don't cuff criers."

Like nothing mattered.
Like he'd never once paid a real price.

▼

WHACK.

"¡Cuántas veces ... te tengo que decir ... que no andes ... con ese

bandolero, come-mierda!"
(How many times do I have to tell you—don't be running with that lowlife, shit-for-brains!)

I scrambled.
Only card left in the deck: Jedi-level guilt trip.[32]

"Al Niño Jesús[33] no le gusta que digan malas palabras."
(Baby Jesus doesn't like it when people curse.)

And for a heartbeat—I saw it.
The flicker.
Her eyes darted to the porcelain Niño Jesús on the shelf—still, glowing faint in the kitchen light, eyes soft like they knew all the family secrets.

I thought: That's it. That's the opening.
Pivot. Diffuse. Salvation via the baby Messiah.

But then—*BAM*.
Another hit. Not out of anger. Out of duty.

"¡Abuelita, te estás pasando!"
(Abuelita, you're crossing the line!)

She didn't even flinch.

---

32 **Jedi-level guilt trip:** A Star Wars nod, likening a guilt trip to a Jedi mind trick—persuasive, disciplined, and cloaked in moral authority. It humorously frames guilt-tripping as near-spiritual manipulation, executed with elite precision.

33 **Niño Jesús:** Spanish for "Baby Jesus." A common religious icon in Latino homes. Danne tries to weaponize innocence against fury—using religion to guilt Abuelita. It nearly works, showing how spiritual imagery doubles as both power lever and cultural guilt trip.

"Mejor un trompón mío que una bala de un policía."[34]
(Better a punch from me than a bullet from a cop.)

And there it was.
Truth—heavy, ancestral,
hard-earned.
Not yelled.
Given.

And just like that, I was ten again.
Standing in her tiny kitchen in socks and shame, wishing I
could fold myself smaller.
Her fury was a front. Her hands, instruments of fear and love
braided tight.
Her words still stung—but now they carved something softer.
A prayer hidden in a slap.

Personally wounded.
But my chest cracked open, just enough for the lesson to sink
in.

She went back to the stove like nothing happened, stirring the
beans with the same hand that struck me.
Steam rose. The smell of garlic and cumin curled in the air.

I sat at the kitchen table, arms crossed, ego still smarting.
She slid a plate in front of me without a word.

▲

---

34 **Better a punch from me than a bullet from a cop:** A Dominican proverb.
It reframes violence as protection. Abuelita's blows aren't abuse but armor. This
line is the emotional core of the chapter: discipline as preemptive mourning.

Later—
I sprawled on my bed, laptop glowing like a digital altar.
Fingers dancing. Code flowing.
A world I controlled. A world that didn't touch me unless I let it.

This was my temple.
My trance. My peace.

Until the door flew open like fate was filing complaints.

In stormed Abuelita—divine judgment in slippers.

She didn't speak until the plate landed in my hands.

"Toma."
(Here.)

One word.
But layered—thick with tone, subtext, and generations of you-better-eat-this-or-else.

Naturally, I poked the bear.

"¿Y algo para tomar?"
(And something to drink?)

Cue the telenovela sigh.

"¡Aaah haa, mira qué lindo! Tiene la comida en la mano y quiere que le traiga algo para tomar también. Tú sí eres. ¿Qué tú te crees, que yo soy tu sirvienta?"
(Oh, how cute! He's got food in his hands and wants me to bring him a drink too. What do you think I am, your maid?)

Still—minutes later—she came back with juice.

•

Because real love shows up, even when it's loud, pissed, and barefoot.

Of course, she couldn't help the parting jab:

"¿Por qué te pasas tanto tiempo en la computadora? Eso da cáncer. Sigue así, tú va' ver, te va' dar un cáncer en la yema." (Why you on that computer so much? That gives you cancer. Keep it up, you'll get cancer on your balls.)

Classic Abuelita.
Her way of saying: I see you hiding. And maybe ... don't.

But her words just ... floated away.
Evaporated in the clink of cheap plastic against my palm.

Juice: fake-sunset orange.[35]
Tasting like a lie you want to believe.

I watched a pulp chunk spiral—slow, aimless.
Like it didn't want to choose a side.

Then—I don't know.

The room tilted.
Not loud. Not dark.
Just off.

Like the air knew where this was headed—and wanted no part of it.

Something in the corner caught the light.
A glint. A shift.

---

35 **Juice: fake-sunset orange:** A poetic metaphor for artificial comfort. The juice isn't just a drink; it's emotional camouflage. A placeholder for affection, care, and the lies we sip anyway because they're familiar.

Like even the shadows were bracing.

I could've looked away.
Could've kept chewing.
Played it safe.

But the question had already landed in my throat.

"¿Dónde está Mami?"
(Where's Mom?)

The room paused. Thick silence.
Eyes flick. Micro-expression.
A crack in the fortress.

"¿Por qué tú preguntas? Tú sabe dónde anda ella. Mira, no
hable tanto y acaba de comer. Quiero que vayas a la bodega."
(Why you asking? You know where she is. Just eat. I need you
to go to the store.)

Conversation: deleted.
But I wasn't done.

"¿Y por qué tú no va'?"
(Then why don't you go?)

I was pushing now.
Testing the perimeter.

She turned—slow.
That look: volcanic, sacred, and not to be messed with.

"Mira que tú ere' atrevido. ¿Tú quiere que te rompa un
diente?"
(Look at you—so damn bold. You want me to knock a tooth
out?)

And somehow—I laughed.

That face?
A weathered map of survival.
Every wrinkle a sermon.[36]

I held her stare—longer than I ever had.

But in the end? I looked down.
Scoop of arroz. Bite of frijoles.

Because some wisdom doesn't come through answers.
It lands in silence.
In the places you're not ready to go yet.

And me? I wasn't winning this round.
Not against Abuelita.

Because in that moment, I wasn't looking for truth.
I was remembering how to survive.

But surviving ... for what?

---

36 **Every wrinkle a sermon:** A metaphor for Abuelita's face. Her body is an archive. This line reminds us that she carries not just memories—but moral instruction. Her skin is a scroll of generational survival.

Chapter Eight

Mucho Dinero

Stanley's Bodega pulsed with its usual evening chaos—
neon buzz, salsa on the radio, and the hum of transactions
stitched together with duct tape and faith.
The air smelled like old coffee, frying oil, and quiet resignation.

Near the back, a girl—ten, maybe eleven—stood at the olive oil
shelf, eyeing a bottle just out of reach.
She stretched. Fingertips grazed glass.
Gravity disagreed.

Enter Chico.
Self-proclaimed guardian of the bodega.
Part-time stock boy.
Full-time pain in the ass.

He spotted her from the freezer aisle—
reaching farther than she should've been able to.

Didn't mean to watch.
But something in her posture—
the poise, the patience—
like she didn't need the world, just the angle.
And for a second, that stopped him.

Chico didn't believe in horoscopes.
Said the planets weren't suggestions. They were systems.
Codes. Divine software still running the operating system of
Earth.
And they didn't whisper. They enforced.

Saturn is the Don Corleone of the group.[37]
Time, endings, contracts.
Lessons you couldn't finesse.
"He don't teach," Chico once said. "He collects."

Mars?
The spark in your blood.
The punch before the apology.
"You feel him in your jaw when you talk back to your mom."

Venus was temptation, yes, but also tax.
"She'll give you everything you want.
Then bill your soul for the craving."

Jupiter, the stormtrooper.
Thunder, expansion, cosmic law.
On Thursdays, Chico wore copper and drank water.[38]
Not to be blessed.

---

37 **Saturn is the Don Corleone of the group:** A metaphorical allusion that
draws a parallel between the Roman god-planet Saturn and Don Vito Corleone,
the commanding patriarch of *The Godfather*. Like Don Corleone, Saturn
embodies power, dignity, and central authority—qualities that elevate it among
the planets through a kind of elegant gravitas.

38 **Copper and water on Thursdays:** In some astrological traditions, each
planet is associated with a metal and a weekday. Thursday corresponds to Jupiter
(linked to abundance and knowledge), and copper is often tied to Venus (love
and beauty). Chico seems to blend these influences.

To understand the invoice.

Mercury? Trickster in a tracksuit.
"Retrograde don't break shit—it reveals what you never fixed."
He ran burner phones. Avoided eye contact with his past.

Chico didn't read charts.
He read residue.

"The sky keeps records," he'd mutter, scanning air like a
barcode.
"Most people too loud to notice."

And when he smiled, that slow buffering smirk—
it wasn't you he was reacting to.
It was Saturn whispering something about your grandmother.

The girl stretched again. This time, Chico moved.

He peeled himself from a fortress of canned goods,
swaggering over like a sheriff in a dusty old Western—
trying too hard to pretend the room agreed with him.

Without a word, he plucked the bottle from the shelf and
handed it to her.

"Thanks," she muttered.

And then—Chico spoke.

"You're welcome. I know you. You're the girl that plays
baseball like a boy."

The words landed like a pigeon aiming for your last clean shirt.

Her grip on the bottle tightened. Shoulders squared.

Her stare wasn't confused; it was calculated.
Like she was running diagnostics.

"Oh, I play like a boy?" she said, tilting her head.
"And you stock shelves like a bitch."

Chico's mouth opened.
Nothing came out.

She turned to leave. But Chico—like an idiot—reached out
and grabbed her wrist.

A power move he hadn't earned.

The second he touched her, she froze.
Not in fear.
Not in hesitation.
In calibration.

She was doing the math—deciding what kind of girl she
needed to be to make sure this never happened again.

Then—she let go of the bottle.

CRASH.

Glass shattered.
Golden oil spilled, thick as blood.
It slithered across tile like it had intent.

A single shard stood upright—
sharp, theatrical, like it was waiting for a line.

Chico stood frozen—center stage in the wreckage.
One misstep from slipping.
One breath from breaking apart.

She stepped back—clean, precise.
Just outside the splash radius.
Watched his face twist in slow realization.

Then she smiled.
Barely.

Didn't run.
Didn't flinch.
Her footsteps didn't rush the door.

Just walked out like she'd checkmated a fool
who didn't even realize they were playing.

"Hey, I was just—"

But she was already gone .

And then—Stanley appeared.

From behind the counter, slow and steady.
Like thunder before the rain.

His eyes scanned the glass, then locked on Chico—
frozen, like a suspect caught mid-crime.

"What happened, Chico?"

His voice was flat.
But the weight behind it pressed like a thumb to the sternum.

"I don't know."

Stanley's brow creased.

"You don't know? Dios mío. That's expensive. Mucho dinero."

Chico stumbled to explain.

"I must've ... blanked out."

"Blanked out," he echoed—
like a lie that didn't even bother to dress up for court.

"Everything's been a disaster since I hired you.
You screw up more than you stock.
I don't even know why I let your dumb ass stay here."

He sighed—heavy.
Rubbed his jaw like checking for old bruises.

Then he dropped it:

"Maybe I just feel bad for your mother."

That hit wasn't loud.
But it echoed.

Silence.

The kind that makes even the ceiling fan hold its breath.

Chico didn't flinch—
but something behind his eyes pulled the curtains.

That's when I stepped in.

Running an errand for Abuelita.
Clocked the scene instantly:
broken glass, oil like a crime scene,
Chico looking like a crash-test dummy after impact.

"Not to interrupt this beautiful bonding moment,
but Abuelita's got a headache. She needs aspirin."

Stanley squinted.

That half-second of distraction was all Chico needed.

"I'll clean it up."

Stanley pointed like he was delivering a sentence.

"You do that. Right now."

I couldn't help myself—muttered under my breath:

"You do that. Right now."

Chico didn't bite.
Just walked to the closet, grabbed the broom, and got to work.

Didn't make eye contact.
Didn't plead.

He wanted to say something—
That maybe if Stanley paid better, he'd get better help.
That maybe he was doing his best.

But his tongue stayed heavy, like it didn't belong to him anymore.

So instead—
he gripped the broom like it was the only thing standing between him and the apocalypse.
Like each sweep might hush the part of him still clawing to scream.

Harsh.
Deliberate.
Each stroke, a confession.

The oil was gone.
But the slick lingered—proof that something had spilled.

Chico kept sweeping.
Not for Stanley.
Not for the money.

But to believe—just once—
that he wasn't always costing more than he gave.

That maybe—just maybe—
someone would stop counting
and finally see him.

Glass scraped the tile like syllables
from a sentence he'd never finish.

Stanley watched. Didn't interrupt.

Just sighed.
Then turned—back to the register.

No more words.

Behind the counter, he rinsed his hands.
Splashed his face.

Like maybe, if he scrubbed hard enough,
the years might let him forget.

▼

If you're wondering why Stanley pressed that rosary
into my grandmother's palm
like a down payment on salvation ...

It's because he owed her. Big time.

She got him his green card.

Fought the paper war with immigration. Dragged his ass
through the system when no one else would.

And worse? She introduced him to his wife.
Sometimes I think he wanted to kill her just for that.
Not because she hurt him—
but because she helped.

Abuelita wore that rosary like a life preserver—
wrapped tight, plastic beads stamped Made in China—
clutched like they came from God herself.

CHAPTER NINE

The Horse & Carriage[39]

Early Wednesday, in the antiseptic purgatory of Dr. Coen's office, Annie—seventeen and Olympic-level indifferent—lounged in an overstuffed armchair like it was custom-built for not giving a damn.

The horse and carriage sat on the desk. Odd thing. Stuck out like a splinter.

Behind her, the scritch-scratch of Coen's pen dragged across paper like clippers chewing through tangled hair—rough, uneven, designed to leave scars.

Annie—man, Annie is that girl.
Combat boots and existential dread.
Pentagrams and ankhs.
Lipstick the color of old wine.
Gothic. Glamorous. Gorgeous disarray.
A contradiction in steel toes.

She'll pull you close just to push you harder.

---

39 **The Horse and Carriage:** Freud likened the psyche to a horse (id/instincts), a carriage (the body), and a driver (the ego, tugged between impulse and reason). In therapy, it illustrates the struggle between chaos and control, a tug-of-war: who's in charge—the wounded self, the mask, or the one making sense of it all?

Starving for validation. Allergic to attention.
She collects anxieties like vinyl. Rare. Fragile. Too easy to
scratch.

And me?
I've got a soft spot for beautiful disasters—
people who burn from the inside
and dare you to touch the flame.

The air thickened.
A pause that wasn't silence.
A signal.

"Why is that horse there?"

The pen stopped.
A flinch. Small. Surgical.

And that's when you'd realize—
it wasn't Coen behind the desk.
It was me.
Danne.
Wearing his shirt. His Freud-wannabe tie. His thick-rimmed
glasses.
I leaned forward, adjusting my posture to match the memory
of Coen slumped here.

"You mean the horse and carriage?"

"Yeah."

Her voice was soft.
But her eyes?
Locked in. Sharp.

I threw up my hands like a magician about to perform psychic surgery.

"Now we're getting somewhere. In short? It represents the body, the essence, and the personality.
Which one you wanna talk about?"

"The essence."

I sighed, like she'd just skipped to the twist in a movie I wasn't done setting up.

"Too soon," I said, shaking my head.
"You can't talk essence without personality.
Can't talk personality without body.
See? We're already sidetracked."

I pointed at the figurine.

"You're here for the same reason that horse is."

"Because my mom's crazy?"

"No, sweetheart. Because of your chihuahua. Then again—yes, your mom. Jesus ..."

Annie had that look—like a book read too many times.
Worn. Underlined. Still holding its spine.

"So," she said, twisting the drawstring on her hoodie, "a week ago, my mom comes home way too early. Walks in and—
boom—there I am, full lip-lock with my girl on the couch."

I raised an eyebrow.
"She didn't know you swung that way?"

Annie leaned back, one foot hooked over her knee.

"Not even a little."

Therapist mode: activated.

"Your girl ... is she the masculine energy in the relationship?"

Annie shot me a look, like I'd just asked if she ran an underground discotheque.

"My girl's binary. Me? Non-binary. If that's what you're asking."

"So you're good with 'she'?"

"Yeah. And for the record? I'm bi. Thought that was obvious."

I nodded, mentally updating the file marked: Approved Pronouns Edition.

"She, he, they—take your pick.
Actually been thinking about ditching 'Annie.'
Maybe go with 'Danni.'"

Danni.

I gave a half-shrug. "If I fumble the pronouns, that's on me. Still learning the terrain."

A smirk. "First step to waking up is realizing you've been sleepwalking, right?"

I grinned. "Touché. Okay—let's get to the meat. What happened after your mom walked in?"

Annie inhaled, slow and steady.
"First off, I didn't have permission to have company over. But there we are—on the couch. And yeah, we're ... naked."

I stared. "Wait. No clothes?"

"Not a stitch."

Her hands trembled—just for a second. Then she clenched them tight, jaw locking like she was swallowing fire.

"Her face flushed tomato-red. Then she lost it. She starts yelling. Calling me tortillera[40] ... and some other things I won't repeat."

My brow furrowed. "What's that mean?" As if I didn't know.

"Tortillera means lesbian."

"And the rest?"

She looked away and bit the inside of her cheek, as if sealing something unsaid.

"Let's just say ... it wasn't kind."

"Fair."
I kept my voice calm. "So how'd you respond? How'd that make you?"

"Told her, 'This is who I am now.'"

I waited.

"She didn't take it well," Annie said. "She grabbed my neck and started to ..."
A breath.
"Started to strangle me."

---

40 **Tortillera:** A harsh, colloquial Spanish slur used to insult lesbians, particularly in Latin American and Caribbean cultures. Its sting isn't just in the word itself but in the way it gets weaponized by family or authority figures— especially when layered with religious shame or gender expectations.

Silence.
The room pulsed around us.

And then—I laughed.
Too loud. Too sudden.
A reflex. A release.
Because if I didn't laugh, I might've drowned in it.

"Wait ... should we be laughing?" she asked.

"Absolutely not!" I wheezed. "Anyway, go on, with your pathetic little story."

"The next day, my mom drops me off at school.
Like nothing happened. And before I slam the door, she says, 'If you get home one minute late—just one—I'm going to hit you again.' And that's when I knew—she still didn't see me."

"What a bitch!" I blurted, no filter.

"When I got back to school, a teacher noticed the ... the ..."

"... strangle marks," I said quietly.

"Yeah. She reported it to the counselor. Counselor called Child Services."

I exhaled. Sharp. Low.

"Wow."

"My mom got arrested. Now I'm in a foster home."

"Seems like everybody got what they deserved."

"You could say that again."

"And how does that make you feel?"

"You want the truth?"

"Always."

Annie hesitated.

"I feel like shit. Like ... not-wanna-be-here kinda shit."

I threw up a hand—reset.

"Nah. We don't say that here."

"But you told me to be real."

"Zip it. Lock it. Throw it away."
I twisted an invisible key.

"Wait—seriously?"

"Zzzip."

"Look, the problem with society is:
Give people a little ear candy and they develop a huge sweet tooth," I continued.

"What?"

"Your body knows the playbook. Move. Hydrate. Feed it like you give a shit.
Fish oil? That's the key.
Smooths out your symptoms. Like nature's Prozac."[41]

---

41 **Fish oil ... nature's Prozac:** A wellness-culture phrase rooted in real but simplified science. Omega-3s (EPA and DHA) may support mood and brain health, but the nickname glosses over the complexities of mental illness. Here, it underscores how institutional care can reduce deep suffering to a supplement list.

"Is that true?"

"Internet says so. Anyway—back to your girlfriend?"

Annie sighed.

"She dumped me right after the incident. Said it made her feel guilty."

I sucked in a breath like I'd been personally betrayed.

"Some people have zero emotional stamina."

"Guess she wasn't ready for the drama."

"But you are. You're still here. That counts for more than you think."

Then—sniffle.
Suddenly misty.

"You okay?" Annie asked.

"I'm good. Just ... skipped breakfast. Blood sugar's low."

She placed her hand on mine.

I took the opening. Intertwined our fingers.

"You just have to keep telling yourself when you miss the bus ... there's always another one coming after it."

She stared like I was a science experiment gone rogue.
Still dangerous. Somehow working.

And just as I was basking in the moment—

BOOM.

The door burst open.

Dr. Coen. The real one.

"Danne! Are you wearing my tie?!"

Locked on me—my pose, my outfit, my hand laced with his patient's.

"And why are you wearing my shirt?!"

I looked down.

"Ah. That explains the starch."

"That's my tie!"
He lunged.
I yanked it off—accidentally smacked him in the face.

"Who's this?" Annie asked.

"He's one of my patients," I said.

"He's one of *my* patients," Coen snapped.

"Wait ... I thought you were Dr. Coen," Annie stuttered.

We both slapped our chests.

"*I'M* DR. COEN!" we shouted.

The real Coen was seething.

"Get. Out. Of. My. Office."

I peeled off the shirt, balled it up, and tossed it at him.

At the door, I turned.

"You stay beautiful, fineness."

SLAM.

Annie stared, half-stunned, half-impressed.

Dr. Coen collapsed into his chair like a man who just watched his ride get towed—with his dignity still in the glovebox.

"I'm ... deeply sorry," he muttered.
"Please disregard everything he said."

"I actually felt good talking to him," Annie shrugged.

"Danne is a deeply troubled individual."

He cleared his throat. Tried to recompose.

"Let's move on. What would you like to talk about today?"

Annie didn't answer right away.

Her eyes drifted to the horse and carriage on the desk.

"Can we talk about that horse?"

He followed her gaze—stared at the figurine like it now held the secrets of the universe.
Let out a sigh—

one of those long, pained ones.
Like he'd just realized he was the carriage—dragged, reins dangling, nowhere near control.

▼

Later, walking away from the scene, it hit me—I was playing a role again. Not just Coen. Not just the outfit.

Maybe I didn't know how to stop.
Maybe I never had.

Worse:
Maybe I wasn't just wearing masks.
Maybe I was making them.
Projecting new realities. Calling it help.

And if I could slip so easy into someone else's skin ...

Maybe there was never anything under mine.

Just layers, stitched too tight to peel off.
Not a self.
Just noise.
Learning how to look alive.

But then again, maybe it's what they needed—
a little chaos, a little fire, someone to smash the mirrors before they got too comfortable.

Maybe that was the point.

CHAPTER TEN

Starving in Public

Later that afternoon, the Hudson stretched in front of us.

It shimmered in the sun like a jazz riff—cool, cagey,
like it only spoke heartbreak in minor chords.

Me and Chico walked the riverbank, our steps just out of sync,
conversation spilling like late-night improv—
part instinct, part misdirection.

"What book you reading now?" I asked, cutting through the
breeze.

"*A Confederacy of Dunces*,"[42] Chico replied—Laurel to my
Hardy.

"Pulitzer, right?"

"Right." His chest puffed like he'd won it himself.

"So ... it's about happy people?"

"It's about people," he said.

---

42 *A Confederacy of Dunces:* A cult novel by John Kennedy Toole featuring
Ignatius J. Reilly, a pompous and delusional misfit. The reference hints at
Chico's affinity for complex, flawed characters—and possibly sees himself in
them.

Which, coming from him, meant: Complicated. Messy. Unknowable.

"Main guy a phony?"

"Not a phony. Just a self-important jackass.
Kinda reminds me of someone I know."

Before I could clap back, Petey crash-landed into our orbit—
pure bedlam in a Yankees cap.
Thirteen, max. Baseball mitt flopping like it was sewn to his arm.

Kid was caught in his own ESPN highlight reel.

"Heads up, Danne! Giambi's rounding third!"

He reenacted Jeter's famous flip,
tossing an invisible ball across an invisible infield.

I dropped into commentator mode:

"Jeter bare hands it—shuffles it to Posada—
aaaaand Giambi is OUT!"

Petey fist-pumped like he'd saved the World Series.

Chico raised an eyebrow.

"Who's the kid?"

"Petey. His pops was a Yankees lifer. Lost him on 9/11."[43]

The silence that followed wasn't empty. It had shape.

---

43 **Lost him on 9/11:** A brief but heavy note tying Petey's father's death to the September 11 attacks. It adds a layer of unspoken grief and shared trauma, grounding an otherwise playful moment in national tragedy.

Like someone holding their breath for someone who never made it back.

Chico shifted gears.

"So ... when am I meeting Rachel?"

His voice had that late-night radio request line energy—equal parts hope and desperation.

"All in good time."

It hung there, heavier than expected.

I nodded.
Mind stalling.
Tongue stalling harder.

I broke the pause with an excuse:

"So I'm officially on the clock, huh?"

Chico groaned like he'd stepped in metaphysical gum.

"You promised, Danne."

"Ah yes—patience unlocks the universe, my son,"
I said, with the gravitas of a fortune cookie on its fifth margarita.

"And here I thought you were just an asshole."

"What's so special about her, anyway?"

"Her ears," he said, dead serious.

"What?"

He hesitated. Then—truth.

"They remind me of calm. Like when someone listens. Really listens."

He looked down, almost like he didn't mean to say that part out loud.

"She looked at me like I was real. Like I wasn't background noise."

I squinted.

"So you're not an ass man. You're an ear man."

He laughed. Soft, but from somewhere real.

"Yeah. And Rachel's? They're perfect.
Especially when they peek out from under her hair.
Like they're listening for something the world forgot to say."

And weirdly? I got it.

"Okay, but if I hook this up, you cannot—*cannot*—start talking about her ears."

"Why not?"

"Because women don't want, 'You've got great earlobes.'
They want, 'Damn, girl, that ass deserves a mural.'"

"I don't say stuff like that."

"Exactly why you're living in the friend zone."

I clapped his back like a shady sensei selling enlightenment door to door.

Then—Chico paused and stop dead in his tracks.

"Let's cross."

"Why?"

He nodded ahead.

Mikey. And his emotional support bully, Moreno. They walked like they owned the city—trouble radiating like cheap cologne.

"Who's the guy?"

"Mikey."

"What're you gonna do?"

"I got this."

"Danne—"

Too late. I stepped into the storm:

"Yo, Mikey. I hear you got beef with Chico."

"Says who?"

"Says Chico. He's tired of you poppin' off. Matter fact, he said if you run your mouth again, he'll knock you so hard your grandkids'll wake up dizzy."

Mikey squinted.

"You a wise guy?"

"Is it true you still suck your thumb?" I added.

His face twitched—like he was flipping through old alibis.

"He said I suck my thumb?"

"And that you wear your mom's heels. Is that true?"

Moreno lit up: "Kick his ass, Mikey!"

I raised both hands.

"Whoa, whoa—if we're talking fights, let's do it right. Gloves. Ref. Neutral ground."

"You his manager now?" Moreno said.

"When?" Mikey asked.

"The seventeenth."

"That's Saturday?" Mikey asked.

"Sunday," Moreno corrected.

"Whatever," Mikey growled.
"Where?"

"The pier," I said.

"What time?"

"Eight A.M. Too early for you?"

"Nah. We got you," Moreno replied.

Just like that, the fight was booked.

As we crossed the street, Mikey threw a final insult at Chico: "Keep-a steppin' ... pussy."

Then Chico turned my shoulder to face him: "I can't believe you just did that."

"You're welcome," I said gleefully.

"I don't wanna fight anybody."

"How you gonna win Rachel if you won't even stand up for yourself?"

"This isn't about Rachel."

"Everything's about Rachel … You ever been with a girl before?"

"That's private."

"You know what this fight's gonna do for you? It's gonna toughen you up. Teach you about rejection. You'll thank me later."

Chico stared at me—the horror slowly dawning.

"So you already knew I was gonna get my ass kicked."

I patted his back, full of brotherly betrayal, and said: "Don't worry, man. It's not gonna hurt … that much."

▼

Then—*BOOM.*
A storm in ripped jeans and flaming kicks.
Diana.

"I texted you thirteen times. Why are you ignoring me?"

"My phone was off."

"You think I'm buying that shit?
Where's my money, Danne?"

"Is this your sister?" Chico whispered.

"Worse. My girlfriend."

"Who's this clown?" she snapped.

"Fran-cis-co," he offered.

"Did I ask you, Fran-cis-co?"

"No."

"You're still talking."

She turned back to me, eyes locked, breathing tight—
like she was holding in more than rage.
Maybe grief. Maybe history. Maybe both.

"I need to go to the salon.
Look at my hair."

"You ever think about cutting it off?
Bet you'd look fly."

"You promised me, Danne. For my birthday.
Don't you see I need these things?"

"And I need you to NOT need these things."

Her eyes flared. Volcanic.
A warning.

Tiny muscles in her jaw flexed.
Stance shifted—fight mode, not flight.

"Fine. Act all macho in front of your little friend,
but don't come crying later."

"Can you not do this in front of my friend?"

"Oh hell no!
If you're picking this freak over me,
go to hell, Danne!"

"Come on, Diana.
Be nice—for once."

She raised her hand.

I caught her wrist—gently, but firm.
Enough to say: not this time.

"Go ahead," she hissed.
"Hit me.
Like your father hit your mother."

Time cracked.

That line didn't just cut;
it tore through me like a double-barrel blast to the chest.

But I swallowed it.

No reaction.
Just reached into my pocket.
Pulled out the wad of cash.

Diana hesitated.
Just for a second.

Her eyes met mine.

Then quick as a thief,
she snatched the whole stack from my hand.

No words.
No thank you.

Just a clean break.

She turned, strutted off—
my dignity tucked under her arm like a designer handbag.

Silence puddled in her wake.

Chico gawked.
Paused.
Then:

"She's got cute ears."

▼

Just when I thought the day had wrung out every last drop of
lunacy,
Leo's car skidded up like karma had the wheel.

"Yo, D, let's go for a ride!" he hollered.

Chico squinted.

"Who's that?"

"You don't wanna know."

Leo didn't have friends.
He had accomplices.
Once you stepped into his orbit, ghosting out wasn't an
option.
It wasn't a hangout.
It was a fraternity of chaos.
The only way in was through the fire.

"C'mon, Danne," Leo grinned.

"I'll take you and your boy out to eat. My treat."

That smile?
Red flag.
The kind your gut clocks before your brain even logs on.

Chico was already nodding.

"Let's go."

"Bad idea."

"Which means it's perfect," Chico smirked.

"Touché."

"Croisé,"[44] he corrected, like he just earned bonus points in a game only he was playing.

"What?"

"Fencing term. Means you take control of your opponent's blade."

I stared—equal parts impressed and mildly concerned.

"Croisé. Brilliant. After you."

"No, after you."

So we slid into the car—Chico up front, me in the back—
and as the tires peeled into the night,
I knew we weren't just boys anymore.

---

44 **Croisé:** A fencing term where one fencer forces the opponent's blade to the opposite line. Chico's casual use of it reveals hidden intelligence and subtle confidence—his own quiet way of taking control in unpredictable situations.

We were co-defendants in a crime that hadn't happened yet.

In the back seat, I clocked a glossy magazine stuffed behind the passenger seat.
"GAY PRIDE," the headline shouted in rainbow bold.

I dangled it into the rearview.

"Yo, Leo. Didn't know you were such an ally."

Leo grinned—
the kind that makes you check your wallet without even moving your hands.

"What can I say? I'm bi-curious."

I eyed the stitching. The wheel. The whole borrowed vibe.

"Leo," I said, voice flattening. "Where'd you get this car?"

"I won it."

"How?"

"Roulette. Atlantic City."

"Oh yeah? What year is it?"

"It's a 2006."

Chico leaned forward, squinting at the dash like a cop on lunch break.

"Looks like an '08."

"You sure you didn't steal it?" I asked.

Leo shot me a look sharp enough to pop a tire.

"What the hell I look like? A thief?"

Silence.
Then—pivot. Smooth as a DJ transition.

"Anyway. I'm throwing a party Saturday. Drinks. Babes. Full send. You in?"

I turned to Chico.

"Can he come?"

Leo shrugged.

"Long as he shaves."

We laughed—stupid, reckless—
rolling toward whatever flavor of purgatory Leo had queued up next.
Life's like Dominican rum—once the cap's off, there's no putting it back. It's built that way.[45]

Inside the restaurant, we moved like rejected extras from a Tarantino flick—
Leo the chaos engine,
Chico the wild card,
and me, the fool who knew better but came anyway.

We slid into a cracked vinyl booth.
Shadows crawled across the table.

45 **Life's like Dominican rum:** A metaphor that mirrors the reckless, intoxicating energy of Leo's world. Once uncorked, it can't be contained— suggesting a lifestyle of thrill-seeking without foresight.

The menus—greasy and warped—held mysteries nobody
wanted solved.

Leo's face twisted mid-page.
"Oh shit ... I only got cash for two meals."
He paused. Let it sit.
Then pointed at Chico.
"So you ain't ordering anything. I'll split mine with you."

"But what if I don't like what you order?"
"You like turkey burgers, right? I'll split mine with you."

Chico hesitated like Leo had just asked him to eat raw drywall.
Chico sighed, already defeated.
"Yeah."
"So I'll get that. Just don't say shit when the waiter comes,
cool?"

Cool.

The waiter showed up—perfect teeth, perfect posture,
too chipper for the low-level fraud
humming at our table.
"What can I get you fellows today?"

"I'll have a chicken quesadilla with a Coke," I said.
Leo: "Turkey burger. Coke."

Waiter turned to Chico.
Chico: "Nah, I'm good."
Leo: "Why don't you get something?"

Chico's eyes lit up.
"Really?"
Leo nodded.

"Claro."

Chico inhaled.

"Okay, I'll have a—"

"Can you give us another minute?" Leo cut in.

The waiter disappeared like smoke.

We were left stewing.

Leo turned to Chico.

"Didn't I tell you not to order anything?"

"But you just said—"

"Don't get smart."

Chico opened his mouth—

but the waiter returned before he could answer.

"You know our orders," Leo said, already sliding back into charm.

"And for you?"

Chico paused. A breath.

"Nothing," he said, steady. "I'm not ordering."

Leo buzzed.

"Not even a little appetizer?"

"Danne, is he playing with me?

"We came all the way to this beautiful restaurant, and you're not ordering anything?" Leo purred.

"I know your tricks, Leo. Not this time."

Silence. Not awkward—just loud.

And this time, Leo didn't grin.

Leo turned to the waiter, already rewriting the narrative.

"His girl ditched him—dude's hurtin' bad."

▼

Moments later, the waiter—clearly seasoned in the high art
of food service dramatics—glided over like he'd trained under
Cirque du Soleil.

With a flourish, he lifted a plate like he was unveiling a sacred
relic.

"A turkey burger."

Leo, ever the showman, puffed up like he just got knighted.

"That's mine," he said, flashing Chico a grin.
"Try not to be too jealous, bro."

With the same reverence, the waiter presented the second act.

"And the chicken quesadilla."

"That's his," Leo nodded toward me like I'd just inherited a
small country.
Then, floating above consequence, he added:
"Oh—and yo, could you hook me up with some water?"

The waiter gave a tight nod.

"Yes, sir. Right away."

Then he vanished, like a magician ducking behind velvet
curtains.

Chico sputtered.
Sat up.

Realization breaking across his face like thunder rolling in.

"Wait—call him back. We need another plate."

Leo tilted his head, innocence smeared across his smirk.

"Why?"

"You said you were gonna split your food with me."

"Yeah, but ... you didn't order anything."

Chico turned to me, eyes wide.

"Danne, didn't he say he'd share?"

I could smell the storm before it broke.

"It's fine, Chico. I'll give you some of mine."

But Leo clapped back fast.

"Nooope. He didn't order. He doesn't eat."

Chico's face crumpled—betrayal, embarrassment, hunger colliding in one deep exhale.

Then he stood.

"Danne, I need air."

I should've said something.
Should've told Leo to quit being a dick.
But I didn't.
Because caring costs more than silence—and I wasn't ready to pay.

And just like that, Chico walked out—shoulders squared like a man heading into weather he didn't have a name for.

Chico wasn't just hungry. He was starving to be seen.[46]
To be chosen.

Through the window, I watched him blur into the city's
background noise—hands in pockets, Leo's bullshit trailing
him like a second shadow.

He passed a woman on the sidewalk.
And for a second, his eyes caught on her ears.
Peeking through her hair like they were listening for
something the world forgot to say.

Maybe we're all starving.
And most days, it's not for food.

▼

Back inside, Leo and I dug in.
Him grinning.
Me chewing.
The moment souring like milk left out too long.

"Damn, this food's delicious," Leo said, twirling his knife like
he was conducting a string section.

"Fancy ass place," I muttered. "Must be expensive."

Leo dabbed his mouth.
Calm as gravity.

"Yeah ... And I can't even pay for it."

---

46 **Starving to be seen:** The phrase turns literal hunger into metaphor:
Chico's need isn't just food; it's for validation, respect, presence. A powerful
encapsulation of how poverty, invisibility, and adolescence can collide.

I choked.

"What the hell do you mean, you can't pay for this?"

"Didn't bring any money."

"You're shitting me."

"Nada."

"So what's the plan, genius?"

"When Chico comes back, I'll start a fight.
They'll toss us. Boom. Free meal."

"That's not a plan."

"We're already driving a stolen car, aren't we?"

My gut dropped.

"You motherfucker. I knew that car wasn't yours."

SLAM.
My hands hit the table just as Chico walked back in.
Oblivious.

"When we leaving?" he asks.

"Soon," I muttered.

"Good. I'm starving."

BOOM.

Leo shot up.

"WHAT THE FUCK?!"

"What?!" Chico froze.

"WHO ATE MY FOOD?!"

"You're joking, right?"

"DID YOU EAT MY FOOD?!"

"Are you psychotic?!"

SLAP.
Knife hits chin.
Tension spikes.

"DON'T LIE TO ME."

The restaurant froze.

The air cracked.

"I'll slit your goddamn throat."

"Danneee, help meee," Chico whimpered.

The waiter returned—palms up, voice calm.

"Sir, if you leave right now, we won't call the police."

Leo paused. Calculated.
Then gently placed the knife on the table.

Clink.

And we ran.
Me. Chico. Leo.
Out the door like hell had just hit the lunch rush.

▲

The city absorbed us like a dry sponge.
Car horns barked.
Neon flickered like cosmic Morse code.
Somewhere in the distance, a siren wailed—a reminder that the
world kept spinning,
indifferent to our madness.

My heart bellowed as me and Chico tore down the block.
And Leo?
That crazy son of a bitch was laughing.

"Hey, guys! Where you going?" he hollered,
his voice laced with amusement—
like a thief watching a tourist fumble with a map.

"HOME!" I barked back, still running.

"C'mon, I'll drive you!"

"WE'RE NOT GETTING IN THE CAR WITH YOU!" I
yelled over my shoulder.

"Why not?" Leo called, still trailing like a kid who just lit a
firecracker.

"It's stolen!" I confessed.

Chico, wheezing, skidded to a stop.
Turned to me, eyes wide.

"I thought he won it gambling?"

Leo gave a shrug so big it belonged on Broadway.

"Gambling, stolen—what's the difference? It's mine now."

"It's not your car, Leo."

Leo just grinned.

"Well, I'm the one driving it."

And in that moment, I swear—
he wasn't just talking about the car.

Leo.
The fox in a city full of sheep.
Moving through life like rules were optional
and consequences were for other people.
He didn't play the game.
He reprogrammed it.

"You're a piece of work," I muttered.

Leo chuckled—slow and smug.
Then, out of nowhere, pulled a fat wad of cash from his
pocket. Peeled off a twenty.
Shoved it into my hand.

"Here. Do me a favor—get this guy something to eat,"
he said, nodding at Chico.
"He's starving."

I stared at the bill like it had betrayed me.

"You had money the whole time?"

Leo grinned like he was about to hand me the meaning of life
in a fortune cookie.

"Gotta roll with the punches, Danne."

I exhaled.
The night.

The adrenaline.
All of it catching up at once.

"Leo, you ever heard of karma?"

His grin only got wider.
Eyes lit with that same reckless, untouchable energy.

"Yeah," he said.
"And she's already in my bed."[47]

And just like that, he was gone—
vanishing into the glowing static of the city,
devoured by the machine he worshipped.

For a moment, there was only silence.

Chico, still catching his breath, let out a sigh—
the kind that sounds like surrender.

"Danne, can I ask you something?"

"If it's about the car, I swear to God—"

"Nah," he said, quieter now.
"Not about that."

I turned. Really looked at him.
My jaw tightened.

I didn't answer.

Chico—
never the type to start shit,

---

47 **Karma's already in my bed:** Leo's final line blends bravado and nihilism.
It suggests he's not afraid of consequence—he courts it. A punchline with bite,
hinting he views fate as something seductive, not fearful.

but always the one left standing in it—
just stared at me, dead serious.

"When am I gonna meet Rachel?"

After all the fire, all the noise,
he still remembered Rachel.

And just like that—the fight, the car, the chaos—
gone.

One word: Rachel. This wasn't just a crush. Not to him.
Maybe not to me either.

I wasn't fooling him or her or myself.

And maybe, just maybe, it was time I stepped out from behind
the sarcasm and let someone see what was left of me.

Chapter Eleven

Morir Soñado (Die Dreaming)

The city drowned in twilight.
Gold and violet spilled into the streets—slow, heavy.
The world wasn't quite here or there.
It hovered.
Caught in that liminal hush
where things lose their names
and become something else entirely.

Streetlights sparked to life
like stars remembering themselves.

Me and Chico strolled through it—
silent observers
in a universe too busy to care we existed.

The breeze snuck between buildings
like a half-remembered thought.
Feral. Familiar. Fractured.

Then—*bam.*
She appeared.
Not a woman.
Something else.

A mirage.
A spell sewn into the last breath of sunlight.

Her skin—molasses-dark, satin-slick—
drank the light like it was communion.
Time's favorite lover.

She moved slow. Certain.
Like she knew the rhythm of the universe and danced to it
while the rest of us fumbled off-beat.

She had the kind of beauty that derails logic.
Dark olive skin that toppled Roman empires,
eyes like the fall of Rome itself.[48]

One look—
your whole kingdom on fire.

I didn't even try to be cool.

"Man, that is some serious ass," I said,
like I was narrating a damn nature documentary.

She kept walking,
eyes locked—
like she knew she was fire
and I was just kindling.

Maybe she was never real.
Maybe she was the echo of something I used to believe in—the
kind of beauty that vanishes the moment you try to name it.

---

48 **Like Rome itself:** This frames beauty as disruptive power, not ornament. By
invoking Cleopatra—whose affairs with Caesar and Antony helped unravel the
Roman Republic—the line ties personal desire to world-altering consequence.
In Danne's world, beauty, memory, and desire are volatile forces.

Maybe that's why I noticed Petey.

Our little orphan shortstop blurring past us—
chasing a father that wasn't there.

Straight into the street. I mean full sprint.
Ghost ground ball.
Bottom of the ninth.
Last-inning save at Yankee Stadium.

All hustle.
No brakes.

Then—a car.

Wrong.
Fast.
Angry.

The world detonated: engine growl, tires shriek,
horn blaring like a pissed off god.

Petey.
Street.
Car.

Run, Forrest, run.[49]

I didn't think. I just moved.
Fingers out. Jersey gripped.
Yanked him back—barely, and I mean barely.

Then—quiet.

---

49 **Run, Forrest, run:** A reference to *Forrest Gump* (1994), where young
Forrest breaks free of his braces and discovers his speed.

He was safe. Breathing.
Me? Still shaking.
My heart was pounding like it was trying to outrun death.

Half a second later, and ...

I exhaled. Sharp. Shaky.

"Hoo. That was close."

Petey stared up at me, like he just cost the Yankees the Series and wanted to go home.

"Danne, can you get my ball?"

I looked around.

"There ain't no ball, Petey."

"Yes, there is."

Chico snickered.
"Just play along, man."

I sighed.
Bent down.
Picked up nothing.

"This it?"

"Not that one."

Another fake grab.
"This one?"

His whole face lit up.

"Yeah! That's it!"

I handed him the nothing.
Shot Chico a look.
He shrugged.

That's the thing about kids:
they haven't been broken yet.
They still see the world as it should be.
Not as it is.

Then I saw it—
Petey's ankle.
Swollen. Angry. Ballooning with bad luck.

I crouched beside him.

"Got some bad news, champ."

His face dropped.

"I can't finish the game?"

"'Fraid not. Might be out for the season."

Tears welled up.
His World Series dreams crumbling
like a sandcastle under tide.

"C'mon," I said, slinging his arm over my shoulder.
"Let's get you back to the clubhouse."

We carried him home—
arms over me and Chico,
his leg floating,
like he still believed
he could make that final play.

And I ain't gonna lie—
I felt a type of way.

Because even after everything the world
had snatched from him,
he still held onto something
I didn't even realize I'd lost.

Something I used to have—
before I learned to duck.
To numb out.
To expect the worst.
Before I mistook pain for purpose.

▲

We stepped into Abuelita's apartment,
and the world softened.

The air—thick with sazón[50] and warm bread—
wrapped around us like a lullaby.

It wasn't just a smell.
It was infrastructure.
Held the whole damn room together.

Me and Chico swaggered in,
laughter skipping across the silence
like pebbles on water.

_____

50 **Sazón:** A staple seasoning in Latinx and Caribbean cooking—typically
coriander, cumin, garlic, oregano, and achiote. It's more than flavor; it's memory
made edible, a symbol of continuity and care that turns Abuelita's kitchen into a
sanctuary against outside chaos.

"Abuelita, traje un amigo. Se llama Chico."
(Abuelita, brought a friend. His name's Chico.)

I called out—tongue in home-mode.

She turned from the stove,
eyes sharp—scanning Chico
like TSA with a grudge.

Chico straightened.

"Mucho gusto, Doña. Me llamo Francisco."
(Nice to meet you, Doña. My name is Francisco.)

Abuelita melted.
Face soft like dough left to rise in a sunny window.

"Mira qué bien. Este sí es buena gente.
Tiene cara de angelito.
No como los delincuentes con quien tú andas."
(Look how nice. This one's good people.
Has the face of an angel.
Not like the delinquents you run with.)

Chico beamed.
I side-eyed.

In that kitchen?
Reality took a coffee break.
Outside was sirens and stolen cars.
Inside?
Sacred.

And with sofrito[51] in the air,
Chico really did look like the angel she imagined.
For a moment—so did I.

Living room: war zone.
Controllers locked.
TV glowing like an altar to ego.

"Wait till you get off the damn ship," I warned.

"Oh really? Just killed all of them," Chico bragged.

"No, you didn't."

"Look who's on the ground."

"There's two people down. Red dots."

"You just want me to die."

"Nah. You just talk so much shit … and you suck."

"Oh yeah?" He grinned. "Then what's that?"

I watched my guy faceplant.

"Look at you," Chico cackled.
"Face-first into the dirt. How's that feel?"

Before I could clap back—footsteps.

Abuelita.

"¿Quieren algo para tomar?"

---

51 **Sofrito:** A sautéed mix of garlic, onions, peppers, and tomatoes,
foundational in Caribbean and Latin American cooking. It represents
inheritance and safety, filling the apartment with tradition and care in contrast to
the danger outside.

119

(Want something to drink?)

I nudged Chico.

"Just say yes. Or she'll keep talking."

"Está bien," he nodded.

She smiled.

"¿Qué le traigo? ¿Morir Soñando?"[52]
(What should I bring you? Die Dreaming?)

And just like that—the world paused.

Her words landed like a melody
from someone who knew your mom
before she got tired.

My tongue twitched with memory.

"Tráenos eso y algo para comer también,"
(Bring us that—and something to eat too.)

Eyes still on the screen,
I added:
"It's important to keep old people busy."

Chico frowned.

"What'd she say?"

I looked over.

---

52 **Morir Soñando:** Literally "to die dreaming." A Dominican mix of orange
juice, milk, sugar, and ice—sweet, creamy, and improbably smooth. In the novel,
it symbolizes fleeting safety and enduring hope, a taste of what Danne once had
but buried.

Kid had Dominican blood but his soul was Wonder Bread.
His mom married a gringo who tried to bleach the sazón out of
him.

He knew more about Budweiser and fireworks
than Brugal[53] or perico ripiao.[54]

"Morir Soñando?" I said.
"It's a drink."

"Yeah, but what's in it?"

I cracked my knuckles.
Ready to preach.

"Fresh OJ.
Condensed milk.
Sugar.
Ice.
Simple—but perfect.
Like heaven in a cup … if heaven had flavor."

Chico lit up.
"Nice."

Morir Soñando.
Yeah, it's a drink. But it's more than that.

---

53 **Brugal:** A well-known Dominican rum, strong and common in island
homes. It marks cultural authenticity versus assimilation—a litmus test of who
carries old-world flavors and who's filtered through Budweiser and fireworks. For
Chico, it signals tension between roots and reinvention.

54 **Perico ripiao:** The original, fast-paced style of Dominican merengue,
powered by accordion, güira, and tambora. Literally "ripped parrot," it carries
a rowdy, rebellious joy. It's more than music—it's survival, resilience through
rhythm.

It's the taste of something you know can't last forever.

And for a moment—with that smell in the air,
with Morir Soñando on its way—
everything felt simple.
Felt safe.

And moments like that?
They're like stolen cars.
Fun while they last.
But you don't get to keep 'em.

The breeze slipped through the window, soft against my
neck—
like it remembered something I'd forgotten.

CHAPTER TWELVE

You Ain't Gonna Believe This...

The sun, slick as a pickpocket, slipped through the blinds in Dr. Coen's office—casting long, snitching stripes across Annie's face.

Another fine Friday,
locked and loaded to grind her dignity into the carpet.

Coen, perched in his overpriced ergonomic throne, opened with the classic:
"How do you feel today?"

"Miserable."

Like he expected applause for remembering the script.

A breeze teased the blinds, like it knew it wasn't welcome but came anyway.
It probably had a podcast and everything.
In this city, even the air had ideas of its own.

Annie shifted in her seat—slow and stiff, like gravity had doubled.

Her silence was its own kind of weather system:
overcast, waiting—charged like storm air.

Dr. Coen nodded like that was exactly what he wanted to hear—
textbook empathy, polished to a sheen.

A reflex more than a response, rehearsed in lecture halls, hollow if you knew where to look.

"There haven't been any changes since we last met?"
"Physically, I'm starting to feel better."

A sliver of optimism clung to her voice,
like a cat skidding across wet tile.

He nodded again.
"Mm-hmm, that's encouraging."

Annie, feeling generous, tossed him a bone.
"It's 'cause of what you told me to do."

He squinted. "What'd I tell you to do?"

"You told me to exercise and take fish oil. Been doing it since."

His brow furrowed—confused.

"That's funny. I don't remember saying that."

"My bad," she said dryly. "Must've been the other Dr. Coen."

A flare passed between them.
Mirror to mirror. Crack to crack.[55]

Silence. Heavy. Awkward. Suddenly religious.

---

55 **Mirror to mirror. Crack to crack:** An image borrowed from Lacanian psychoanalysis and myth: the mirror stage as a site of both recognition and illusion. When two fractured selves confront each other, the reflection isn't truth; it's tension held in symmetry.

Coen's face twisted like he'd just tasted warm milk.

"There is no *other* Dr. Coen. I'm Dr. Coen. It's probably best you purge everything he told you—for your own good."
Coen shifted like the world was on his back—and maybe not worth it.

Trying to break the tension, Annie lobbed a curveball.
"Can I ask you something?"

Coen sighed, already regretting it. "By all means."

"Usually I'm good with names and faces, but ..."

"Let me guess—my name doesn't match my face? Dad's Jewish. Mom's Jamaican."

Annie nodded, absorbing it.
"That makes sense. You carry both like you were born to."

Coen gave a tired smile, then let something slip.
"I guess I had to. And I got bullied for it."

He exhaled.

"Kids didn't hold back. My skin color was their favorite joke—
'Looking white today, Coen!'
or 'Having a Black day, are we?'"

Annie pulsed, scandalized. "That's horrible."

He shrugged—muscle memory.
"One time they passed around a drawing—kid's face on a zebra's body. My name underneath."

Should've framed it. Honestly, that's creativity.

Before the moment could settle, Annie fired again.
"Mind if I ask you one more?"

Coen, already running on fumes: "Sure, go ahead."

She tilted her head toward the window.
Light caught her eyes—just enough to see what was waiting.

He followed her gaze.

Then—
like a thought she didn't remember thinking—I was there.

I was crouched above the door, face smashed to the narrow
glass like a nosy Spider-Man with boundary issues.
One of those windows nobody ever looks at—unless they're
being robbed.
The blinds jittered against the frame, a nervous metronome
ratting me out.

"Is he supposed to be here?" Annie asked.

Coen's demeanor froze. The office held its breath.
No longer a place of healing—
but a stage in disguise, poised for judgment.

Not the look of a man caught off guard but of a mask cracking
beneath the lights.
The kind of stillness that settles when illusion realizes it's been
seen.

"No, he isn't," Coen muttered,
his voice fraying like a lamp about to short.
But he tried to play it cool.
He tossed out a nervous chuckle like it cost nothing—just

spare change.

"Danne's ... a unique case. Just ignore him, and he'll go away."

He was wrong.

I turned from the window, a smile creeping despite the tension, wondering how much sweat was hiding behind Coen's calm.
Then, pulling out the office key—stolen, obviously—
I let myself in like I owned the building.
Technically, I only owned the audacity.

Coen bolted upright.
"You can't be in here!"

"No offense, Doc—
but you're full of shit."

I turned to Annie, like a game show host about to change her life.

"You ever wonder why he talks so much?
He's in love with the sound of his own brilliance—
his ideas get him off."

Then I turned my gaze to him and said,
"Doc, everything's shifting. Right now. And you don't even see it. We're plugged in 24/7—scrolling, spiraling—and calling it connection when it's submission."

Two new gods are being marketed to the masses.[56]

The first moves hand-to-hand through initiates: psychedelics—not to escape, but to prepare. What's coming isn't a trip; it's a takeover.
This first god trains the mind to loosen its grip, to get ready.

The second doesn't come in visions; it comes in code.
It speaks in algorithms. It thinks faster than prayer.
Superintelligence—not the future, but the now.

And we are already bowing.
We just call it convenience.

We think we're in control, but we kneel—not with reverence, but with exhaustion.

Every click, swipe, and whispered command to a black glass screen is a quiet genuflection, a pilgrimage to a new Black Stone:[57]
cold, coded, set not in sacred Earth but in circuits and desire.

---

56 **Two new gods are being marketed to the masses:** This line casts psychedelics and artificial intelligence as modern spiritual movements. The first, rooted in Indigenous rituals but rebranded in wellness culture, expands consciousness. The second—superintelligence—embodies algorithmic power. Together, they promise revelation and control, prophecy and its engineering.

57 **The New Black Stone:** In Mecca, the Black Stone marks the Kaaba's corner, anchoring the ritual of ṭawāf. Not an idol but a center, its mystery—possibly meteorite, possibly relic—deepens its spiritual weight. The metaphor reframes this power: today's "new Black Stone" is the smartphone, a sleek cube we orbit daily. One anchors cosmic devotion, the other digital dependence. Sacred geometry becomes user interface; stone becomes screen. The Kaaba aligned the faithful; now the algorithm aligns the user. We haven't stopped worshiping—we've only changed what we bow to.

We trade sovereignty for speed, discernment for ease, until choice itself becomes a ghost in the machine.

"And you're still running the same old playbook, trying to map a dying world onto a new one that doesn't even care about the rules.

You're not wrong.

You're just late."

Coen damn near swallowed his tongue.
"Annie, our session is over."

His hand jittered across the desk, knocking over a cup of pens.
Then, turning to me:
"And I want you out."

I ignored him like a Jehovah's Witness at the door.

"Annie, are you heartbroken?"

"That's none of your business!" Coen barked.
"Don't answer that!" he snapped at her, voice laced with desperate professionalism.

Annie shifted in her seat, visibly rattled.
Her sneaker scuffed against the carpet—a small, helpless noise.

Her gaze bounced between us. Her hands trembled.

Something inside her wobbled—not breaking yet but bending toward it.

Then, with a tight sigh, she muttered,
"I should leave."

"Yes," Coen said, nearly shouting.

But before she could bolt, I grinned.
"You're welcome."

Then I turned back to Coen, poised and predatory.

"Hey Doc, you know the difference between a white fairy tale and a Black fairy tale?"

His eye twitched.

"Danne, don't—"

Coen flinched, hand jerking up like a man about to drown.

But I didn't stop.

"A white fairy tale starts with 'Once upon a time.'
But a Black fairy tale starts with:
'Yo, you muthafuckas ain't gonna believe this shit.'"

Coen sparked—once, twice—like his soul needed to buffer.

Then—
"GET. THE HELL. OUT!"

I tossed him a wink.
"Don't worry, Doc. I'll lock the door on my way out."

Filed under: doctors who meant well, but missed the exit.

The room exhaled behind me: a pile of leather-bound delusions, a young woman with her storm still gathering, and one man Googling early retirement like it was salvation with a dental plan.

CHAPTER THIRTEEN

Ashes Don't Apologize

Late Friday afternoon.
The world was peeling off its workweek skin, already halfway into a greasy, pleasure-soaked weekend. And right in the middle of it all—Ft. Washington Park. A decent place to get lost.

But Annie wasn't lost.
She was vibin'.
Taking the scenic route home, her steps drumming out a beat only she could hear.

Meanwhile, behind her—something red kept flickering in and out.
Red sneakers.
Bouncing like a Broadway understudy desperate for stage time.

Annie smelled bullshit the way rats smell free food.
That supernatural female instinct—the one that can spot a side chick off two likes.

She paused. Turned. Gone.
Red sneakers had vanished like a whisper nobody trusts but everybody hears.

She stopped. The sneakers stopped.
She turned. They disappeared.
She walked. They came back.

By spin number three, it was full-blown Looney Tunes meets
Law & Order.
The sneakers were playing peekaboo with her paranoia—
leaping in and out like Houdini on Red Bull.

So Annie cut the nonsense.
Dipped behind a wall. Waited.

And when my dumbass strutted past—chest out like I paid
rent on the whole block—*BOOM.*
She popped out like a repressed memory with a vendetta and
smacked me on the shoulder with full parole officer energy.

I stumbled, breath snatched clean outta my lungs.
"I'm right here, dummy."

Her face? Two syllables away from handing me an ass
whooping.
I flinched so hard I almost threw my back out.

"Yo! You tryna kill me or what?"

She squinted like she was trying to read the fine print of my
stupidity.
"Why you creepin' like that?"

I cleared my throat. Straightened up like I was in court.
"Just makin' sure you good."

Her eyebrows flew north, probably lookin' for Jesus.
"Aww. How sweet."

"What'd you think about my little stunt at Coen's office earlier?"

She gave me a sideways glance.
"Depends."

"On what?"

Her tone shifted.
"On whether you actually care ... or just tryna slide in close."

I put my hands up, all innocent.
"Chill, it ain't like that. I ain't even into you like that—"

She cut in.
"Wow. So I just got hit with the 'you cute but not for me' special?"

"Nah, it ain't that. I just can't stop thinkin' about you and your moms wildin'."

Annie wavered—like I'd just said pineapple belongs on pizza.
"You don't say."

"I keep runnin' it back—your mom bustin' in, screamin', scratchin', blood everywhere."

She folded her arms.
"And you tellin' it like it's your bedtime story."

"If I was your moms? I'd have handled that beatdown smarter."

She tilted her head. Half-curious. Half-ready to slap.
"Enlighten me, Sensei."

I leaned in, grinning.
"I'd grab a nylon, stuff it with oranges, and wear you out 'til it

snapped."

"Oranges?" she repeated. Not sure if I was a genius or a menace.

"Yeah. Oranges don't leave marks. Not even strangle marks."[58]

"Wow. Remind me to keep my fruit bowl locked up."

"Kills you kindly. Leaves no trace but juice."

"You're sick, you know that."

"I'll take that as a compliment."

Annie shook her head.
"You a whole idiot."

I broke into Dr. Coen's signature laugh.
Annie cracked first. Then I lost it.

Both of us doubled over—laughing like the world couldn't touch us.
For one breath, it almost felt safe.

Then, the universe coughed up its punchline.
Diana.

Popped up outta nowhere—like an overdue bill or a roach that just won't die.
Tiny Pomeranian trotting beside her, tail wagging—completely

---

58 **Oranges don't leave marks:** A reference to an often-cited (but medically debated) urban legend: that a beating with a sock filled with oranges won't bruise the skin, making it a "trace-free" weapon. Its use here is both darkly comic and viscerally charged—mirroring intergenerational trauma wrapped in folklore and survival strategy.

unaware his owner was about to burn my life to the ground.

Diana froze mid-step.
Her eyes ping-ponged: Me. Annie. Me again.

Just like that—I became a corpse.
"Well, well, well ... so this is why you couldn't see me yesterday?"

I scrambled.
"Diana, it's not what you think!"

She huffed so hard, birds fled the trees.
Then turned to Annie, scanning her like TSA at JFK.

"So *this* is what you like now, huh? I can do goth. I can do goth like nobody can do goth."

Annie squinted. Unfazed.
"Does she go to our school?"

Diana's head whipped back.
"SHE has a NAME. And she goes to PRIVATE SCHOOL, THANK YOU VERY MUCH."

Annie nodded.
"Yeah. I can tell."

Diana's nostrils flared like a dragon about to roast me.
"SAY SOMETHING, DANNE. SAY SOMETHING RIGHT NOW."

I shrugged.
"Please forgive her. She didn't take her meds this morning."

Dead. Silence.

Diana's soul crashed like a video file with its metadata stripped—there but unreadable.
Her eyes still played the scene, but the tags were gone: no name, no timestamp, no authorship.
Just raw, silent playback. Like she'd let me in, then deleted the part where I mattered.

"Ohhhh, THAT crack is gonna cost you BIG TIME."

Annie backed up like the air had turned against her.
"I think I should go."

I panicked.
"No, don't go!"

Diana gasped like I'd just proposed marriage.
"HAH! I CAN'T BELIEVE YOU JUST DID THAT."

I trembled.
"Did what?"

"SUBCONSCIOUSLY, YOU PICKED HER OVER ME."

I groaned.
"Diana, that's ridiculous. She's just a friend from school."

Diana's arms flailed like she was signaling an airstrike.
"THAT'S HOW IT STARTS, DUMMY."

I lowered my voice.
"Diana, please. You're embarrassing me. Can we talk about this later?"

Diana's face did that villain-smirk-before-the-bomb-goes-off thing.
"No. There IS no later.

It's OVER, Danne.

Don't call me. Don't text me.

Don't even come over unless you wanna walk into a CRIME SCENE.

TO THINK I wasted all my mobile minutes on you!"[59]

Diana wasn't the type to storm off quietly.

She scorched the earth and let the silence sort out the survivors.

She was already typing as she walked—thumbs moving like assassins.

A selfie went up first. Eyes wet. Lashes perfect.

Caption locked and loaded: "Love the aesthetic, fear the commitment."

Then came the real warheads: Screenshots. Old flirty messages.

Maybe even that crying voice memo I sent last winter.

She knew which grenades to pull.

Knew which friend groups would turn fastest.

Knew the hashtags that hit hardest.

And the worst part?

I deserved every bit of it.

Just like that, it hit me —

The night she sat outside my building 'til sunrise.

No text. No call. Just presence.

---

59 **Mobile minutes:** A throwback phrase referencing when cell phone plans charged by the minute, especially for calls outside certain hours. Diana's outrage is steeped in a kind of nostalgic Gen Z–Millennial crossover trauma—the joke lands hardest if you remember budgeting emotional breakdowns around peak-hour billing.

When I finally came down, she handed me a Gatorade and said, "You look like hell."

I didn't even deserve the Gatorade.

I threw it all away—her quiet loyalty, her fear, the kind of care you don't earn twice—for a laugh.
For a thrill. For something too empty to even name.

Still don't know what I was chasing.
But I feel every inch of what I lost.

Then—the final blow.

Annie turned to me, smirking like Loki about to monologue.
I just stood there. Ash in my mouth. Blood in my ears.
The street was quiet. Even the wind held its breath.

I opened my mouth. Nothing came out.

"You know what they say, Danne—when you miss the bus..."

A pause. Then:
"There's always another one coming after it."

She winked.
Not cute. Not coy. Like she'd seen the ending already—and figured out I was just the trailer, not the movie.

CHAPTER FOURTEEN

Monument Park

Late afternoon sat heavy on our building—
like an uneasy truce that wasn't gonna hold.
That kind of golden hour where everything looks loaded, like
it's waiting to speak.

Twilight slithered through cracked blinds and under
doorways—
smooth as a late-night hacker.
Twice as sneaky.

It wrapped the hallway in a faded yellow haze that smelled
faintly of mop water, burnt rice, and somebody's over-dried
laundry.
I moved slow, like the shadows might jump if I startled them.
Not quite paranoia—more like that ache when you know
someone's watching.
Even if it's just the building itself.

Not paranoia.
More like the feeling when you realize you've stopped existing
in other people's eyes.
And maybe in your own.

The day's drama still rattled around in my skull—

sharp corners, endless iterations.
And I couldn't shake it.

That feeling again—like the air had eyes and a grudge.
Not metaphorically. Really watching.
Like the hallway had secrets, and I was the only idiot who
didn't get the memo.

As I walked, Diana's face flashed through my mind—
how fast things had gone from zero to disaster.
No time to explain.
No time to fix it.

But this wasn't about her. Not now.
I was still stuck in the aftermath,
trying to make sense of everything,
one weird encounter at a time.

Then—*bam.* That prickle.
The one that crawls up your neck when the universe is about
to mess with you.

I spun. A clean 180.
If I'd had skates on, I'd have taken gold in the Paranoia
Olympics.

Caught you, creeper.

But instead of a demon, serial killer, or federal agent ...
Olive Oil Girl.
Pint-sized chaos gremlin from the bodega.
The one who almost turned aisle three into a Slip 'N Slide.

She peeked from behind her apartment door—
a tiny agent of mischief wrapped in stickers and suspicious

energy.

She flinched when she saw me—
like she'd been caught smuggling state secrets.
But that look? That wide-eyed smirk?

Yeah. She was absolutely spying on me.
And I wasn't about to let that slide.

I stalked up to her door like I was serving a warrant.
One ring.
Then two.
Then one more—just to be petty.

Inside, Olive Oil Girl was spiraling.
Her heartbeat was loud enough to file a noise complaint.
She probably thought I rolled in with backup and a manila
folder with her name on it.

She tiptoed to the door like a raccoon avoiding motion sensors.
Peeked through the peephole ...
Nothing.

I'd ducked out of frame like a nosy neighbor with a vendetta.

She bit her lip. Peeked again.
Still empty.
She cracked the door open—slow as molasses and—

BOO.

I popped out like a fart in hot yoga.
No scream—just pure betrayal in her eyes,
like I was the reason NBC canceled her favorite show.

Now fully exposed under hallway light, she stood there—

Yankees tee one size too small, washed so thin it had the self-esteem of a turtle in gym class.
Scowl locked and loaded.

I hit her with the look—
channeling every detective from every cop show my grandmother ever binged.

"What're you doing?"

She fluttered, all innocence.
"Nothing."

Uh-huh.
I squinted.
"Don't play with me. You spying on me?"

She didn't even crack. Came back quick, fast, and savage:
"No. My mom says you're not ... normal."

Damn.
That hit harder than a group chat roast.

I paused.
Adjusted my pride like it was sagging jeans.

"Oh, word? Well, guess what people say about you?"

She tilted her head, suspicious.
"What?"

I leaned in. Lowered my voice.
"That you play baseball ... like a *boy*."

Her lip twitched.
Oh, she felt that.

Then slowly—too slowly—she smirked.
"Nah. I play baseball like a girl."

Then came the knockout punch:
"I'm just *better* than all the boys."

I backed up, hands raised.
I'd been cooked.
Barbecued.
Served with humble pie and no sides.

"A'ight. What's your name, slugger?"

"Martina."
Said it proud like she invented it.

I nodded at her Yankees tee.
"Lemme guess—Derek Jeter fan?"

Her face lit up like Times Square on Halloween.
"Duh! Best Yankee ever."

"Better than DiMaggio?"
"Played longer."

"Gehrig?"
"Weak era. No Black players."[60]

"Babe Ruth?"

---

60 **Weak era. No Black players:** A subtle but sharp critique. Lou Gehrig played in the 1920s–30s, before MLB's racial integration in 1947. Martina's comment isn't just sass; it's historical awareness. She isn't dazzled by stats without justice; she reads greatness through access.

"Red Sock in disguise."[61]

I flared.
This kid was surgical.

"Mickey Mantle? Twelve World Series. Won seven."

She rolled her eyes.
"Last four years were trash.[62] And besides ..."

She paused—delivering this like it came straight from the mountaintop.

"Derek's cuter."

Now I was just getting bullied.

"Yogi Berra? Ten rings. Most decorated Yankee."

Martina paused.
Finally—finally—chewed on it.

Then, with the confidence of a kid who just dunked on a grown man:
"Yogi comes close. But Jeter's got something he never had."

I raised an eyebrow.
"What's that?"

---

61 **Red Sock in disguise:** Babe Ruth famously played for the Boston Red Sox before being sold to the Yankees—a move that triggered the so-called "Curse of the Bambino." Calling him a "Red Sock in disguise" isn't just shade; it's heresy for Yankee fans. Martina's line flips sports mythology into comedy.

62 **Last four years were trash:** Mantle's later seasons were statistically weaker due to injuries and age. Martina's line shows a stat-savvy eye, calling out the decline in contrast to his legend status. She respects truth over reputation—and isn't afraid to say it.

She leaned in. Eyes glittering.
"He's got that watch."[63]

And just like that ...
I was done.
Just for a second, I let the armor slip.

She didn't just beat me.
She benched me.
Then buried me in Monument Park.[64]

I walked back down the hall, a little slower than before.
Monument Park isn't just for legends anymore.
Maybe it's for survivors, too.

Martina was younger, shorter, and smarter—
and somehow, more real than most grown men I knew.

Her words hit like a sniper's shot: clear, deliberate, cutting through all the noise.
She wasn't out here trying to prove anything; she didn't have to.
It was the kind of confidence that didn't need validation—
the kind that made her bulletproof.

---

63 **But Jeter's got that watch:** Yogi Berra may be the greatest Yankee on paper—10 rings, 18 All-Star nods, and timeless "Yogisms." But Martina isn't citing stats; she's citing style. Jeter's Movado watch signals curated cool, a brand still alive in her generation, while Yogi's greatness feels archived in grainy footage and myth. It's not disrespect, but generational drift: aura over numbers.

64 **Monument Park:** Located inside Yankee Stadium, Monument Park honors the team's greatest players with plaques and retired numbers. Here, it's also used metaphorically—as a place not just for legends but for survivors. A subtle nod to resilience as its own legacy.

But it wasn't just that.
She reminded me of someone—someone I used to be.
She had that edge, that sharpness that comes when you've had to fight for respect since day one.

It was like watching a younger version of myself in a different skin.
And I wasn't sure if I was proud of her—
or intimidated.

Maybe both.
Maybe that's the real Monument Park.

CHAPTER FIFTEEN

Scylla, Charybdis, and Rum

I stomped into the apartment like Odysseus caught between
Scylla and Charybdis[65]
except my monsters were teenage heartbreak and Abuelita's
unsolicited wisdom.
The kind of wisdom that waits for you to hit rock bottom ...
then offers you a pillow.
She was out cold on the couch,
the TV scanning her face like it was looking for signs of life.
Didn't even stir when I walked in.
Unacceptable.

I needed an audience for my misery.
So I dropped my keys on the table like a break shot—
shattering the silence in half.
A move made to be heard, not answered.
She jolted awake with a half-snore, half-curse,
gleaming at me like I'd just kicked in the door.

---

65 **Scylla and Charybdis:** In Homer's *Odyssey*, Scylla and Charybdis are
mythical sea monsters Odysseus must navigate between—one a rock-dwelling
beast that snatches sailors, the other a whirlpool that swallows ships. The
reference here sets the tone for Danne's no-win emotional trap: between
heartbreak and generational fire.

"¿Mami no ha llegado todavía?"
(Mommy hasn't come home yet?)

I knew the answer. I just needed to hear it.
She smacked her lips, still halfway between dream and novela.

"Tú sabes la vida que ella vive. Siempre está en la calle con sus novios."
(You know the life she leads. Always out in the streets with her boyfriends.)

I let out a bitter laugh—
silent, sharp.
The kind that feels like screaming without the sound.

"¡Con-yo, ella nunca está aquí cuando la necesito!"
(Fuck, she's never here when I need her!)

Abuelita quivered, slow and deliberate.
"¿Qué tú quieres que yo haga, mijo?"
(What do you want me to do, baby?)

She sat up, adjusted her house dress,
and locked in with that Abuelita glare
that could make grown men confess to crimes they didn't commit.

"¿Qué te pasa?"
(What's wrong?)

I waved her off.
Nothing.
Which, of course, meant everything.

She didn't move.

Didn't stir.
"Dímelo a mí. Yo te escucho."
(Tell me. I'll listen.)

I scoffed.
"No, tú no puedes entender esto."
(No, you wouldn't understand this.)

Because if I started,
I wouldn't stop.
And if I didn't stop ...
I might say something I couldn't take back.

I stormed off—
like the bathroom was a baptism.
Spoiler: it wasn't.

Slam.
Lock.
Safe.

Outside, I heard her pacing.

"¿Qué te pasa, mi cielo? Tuviste una pelea con Diana? Olvídala,
ella no vale la pena."
(What's wrong, my love? You fought with Diana? Forget her.
She's not worth it.)

I ignored her.
I knew what I was doing.
I just—
didn't know how to stop.

And then—*BOOM.*
I shot out of the bathroom like my ass was on fire,

149

locked in on the kitchen like it owed me salvation.
Sweet, terrible rum—
because therapy takes too long.

"¿Tú piensas que eres el único con el corazón partido?
Mijo, todo el mundo lo ha sentido. Madura."
(You think you're the only one with a broken heart?
Baby, everyone's felt it. Grow up.)

I yanked the cabinet open
like it was hiding the last truth on Earth.
Snatched the bottle from exile,
twisted it open like peeling off my own skin.

The cap spun across the counter,
did one Olympic twirl,
and thunked like a drunk ballerina bowing out.

Perfect landing.
Destructive grace.

By the time Abuelita caught up,
I had the bottle in hand like a threat
and locked myself in my room.

Her eyes went wide.

"¡No me digas que te vas a destruir la vida por esa muchacha!"
(Don't tell me you're gonna ruin your life over that girl!)

Still nothing.

Then—switch flipped.
She went full Godfather.

"Mira, ya no jodas más y abre la puerta."

(Look, stop fucking around and open the door.)

I didn't flinch.
Held my ground.

Because sometimes silence screams louder than words.

The silence pressed against the door like it wanted in, too.
She leaned in—her voice now smoke and thunder:

"¿Tú sabes cuántas mujeres hay en este mundo?
¡MUCHÍSIMAS!"
(You know how many women there are in this world? A LOT!)

Still I stood there,
heat rising behind my ribs like a busted radiator.

"¿Tú quieres que saque el bate? ¿Eso es lo que tú quieres?
¡CABRÓN!"
(You want me to get the bat out? Is that what you want?
ASSHOLE!)

I sipped the rum—
half drunk,
half impressed.

Then—nuclear launch initiated:

"DANNE, SI NO ME ABRES, VOY A LLAMAR EL
PSIQUIATRA!"
(Danne, if you don't open this door, I'm calling the
psychiatrist!)

And just like that—
she marched off,
dialed up Dr. Coen like he was Ghostbusters

151

and I was the poltergeist with emotional issues.

Her voice—raspy, raw, soaked in Catholic guilt—spilled through the line:

"Perdona que le estoy llamando tan tarde ..."
(Forgive me for calling so late ...)

She said it like I was in the kitchen
whipping up a cocktail called The Abuelita Coma Special—
one part sleeping pills,
two parts Dominican rum,
and a splash of I've-made-a-huge-mistake.

Every syllable of my name wrapped around my throat like a noose.

I stepped out of my room, heart pounding.
Abuelita stood there,
phone clutched like it was Jesus' hotline,
cord wound tight like she was choking the devil out of it.

"Mira, Danne. Tengo el doctor en la línea. Habla con él."
(Look, Danne. I have the doctor on the line. Talk to him.)

Some part of me still wanted her to save me.
But I didn't know how to let her.

Her tone was soft. Deceptively soft.
That grandma-soft right before she slaps you in the back of the head.

I moved past her—
heavy-breathing, hormone-fueled, full-blown rage goblin.

The cupboard slammed open.

I snatched the pill bottle like I was winning a reality show.

SLAM.
I dropped it on the counter like a gun cocking in a quiet room.

Abuelita flinched.
She started praying to every saint from
La Virgen de la Altagracia to San Miguel.[66]

"¿Por qué tú no hablas con él y te desahogas de todos tus sufrimientos?"
(Why don't you talk to him and let go of all your suffering?)

Her voice went full Lifetime movie—
like someone just got amnesia again.

She was good. But I was better.

I snatched the phone.
It was warm in my hand—like her grip had left something behind.
I looked at her.
Then the phone.

If I let her in now,
I'd have to admit I needed saving.
And I couldn't afford to be that boy tonight.

I looked at her again.

---

66 **La Virgen de la Altagracia / San Miguel:** La Virgen de la Altagracia is the patron saint of the Dominican Republic, often prayed to for protection and guidance. San Miguel (Saint Michael) is the archangel who leads heaven's armies and is invoked for strength against evil. Abuelita's prayer pulls from deep, ancestral Catholic tradition—her response is spiritual warfare cloaked in maternal fear.

She didn't flinch.
Neither did I.

Then—sharp enough to shatter windows—
"Fuck you."

And for a second, the whole world held its breath.

That was it.

Abuelita's hand flew to her chest like I'd sucker-punched Jesus.

She didn't speak.
Just stood there, holding her breath like I might hand it back.

Chapter Sixteen

The Gospel According to the Fool

Saturday morning light tiptoed in, careful not to wake
Abuelita—
sprawled on the couch like a prizefighter between rounds,
knocked out cold from last night's rumble.
Morning wasn't an adult yet.
It was still a toddler—restless, clumsy, knocking over the
wreckage of what came before.

And then I appeared.
Your friendly neighborhood train wreck.
Flashing out of the corridor into the blaze of daylight like a
man unfamiliar with mornings.

My face? A crime scene.
My hair? Looked like a raccoon had been nesting in it.
My voice? Gravel.

"¿Qué hora es?"
(What time is it?)
I croaked, like some aging pirate waking from a rum coma.

"Son las doce del día," Abuelita grumbled, eyes barely cracking
open.
(It's noon.)

Noon.
That unforgiving hour that slaps you with the truth:
you wasted half a day being a dumbass.

And then I saw it—the tired slump in her shoulders,
the exhaustion braided into the wrinkles on her forehead.

"¿Qué te pasa?" I asked.
(What's wrong?)

"Tuve una pesadilla anoche."
(I had a nightmare last night.)

She dreamt she was drowning—alone, thrashing in the sea's
wrath, while I stood safely on the shore, just watching her drift
away.

A guilt trigger disguised as a bedtime story.

Her words lingered—heavy, sharp, designed to bypass logic
and hit me straight in the gut.

"Mira, Abuelita ... ya no tienes que preocuparte más. Diana y
yo terminamos ayer."
(Listen, Grandma ... you don't have to worry anymore. Diana
and I broke up yesterday.)

Relief burst across her face so fast
I thought she might break into hymns.

"¡Qué bueno! Si ella llama otra vez, la voy a mandar al carajo."
(That's wonderful! If she calls again, I'm sending her straight
to hell.)

Wait. Rewind.

"¿Diana me llamó?"
(Diana called me?)

"Sí."
(Yes.)

I sparked.
Neurons scattered like mice in a kitchen.

"¿Y por qué no me despertaste?"
(Why didn't you wake me up?)

She hit me with the Abuelita Glare™—the kind that could
spoil milk and turn bones to ash.

"Bah, muchacho del diablo ... ¿es que te estás volviendo loco?
Me dijiste que terminaron y ahora me estás preguntando si ella
te llamó ..."
(You little devil ... are you losing your damn mind? You just
told me you broke up and now you're asking if she called?)

Maybe.
If going back to her was a mistake, it was one I'd made enough
times to stop calling it a mistake.
At this point, it felt more like muscle memory than madness.

I had no comeback.
Just one thought doing donuts in my brain:
What the hell did she want?

"Hello? Diana? My grandmother said you called."

She had.
And she hadn't left a message.

That should've told me everything.

Instead, I let it tell me what I wanted.

She called.
That had to mean something.
Even if it didn't, I decided it did.

Sometimes, the story you tell yourself is all you've got.

Outside, Abuelita sighed the sigh of generations—
long, disappointed, and practiced.

She got up like she'd aged three decades, and solved a murder in
the process.

Then she did what all great matriarchs do:
grabbed her broom and started scrubbing the apartment clean
of last night's sins.

Dustpan. Mop. Santo Rosario on standby.[67]

By the time I re-emerged from the shadows, I'd undergone a
full-blown transformation.
The idiot was gone—overwritten by a man running a new
script: one line of purpose, a hundred lines of denial.

I stood there—suited up.
Black blazer, red sneakers—teenage rebellion caught mid-
sentence.

I flipped through *48 Laws of Power* like it was a crooked

---

67 **Santo Rosario:** The Holy Rosary is both a set of prayers and the beads used
to recite them. For many Latine matriarchs, it's more than ritual—it's defense
and devotion. When Abuelita takes it up, she isn't just tidying the apartment
but resetting it spiritually. The rosary becomes weapon, balm, and recalibration,
casting her as a domestic priestess who believes emotional chaos leaves residue—
and knows how to cleanse it.

therapist—one with perfect hair and no moral compass.

Diana's name wasn't on the page,
but it might as well have been watermarked into the margins.

I wasn't going to beg.
I wasn't going to explain.
I was going to win.
(Even if I didn't know what that meant anymore.)

Still, I scrawled a note:
Find her weakness before she bleeds mine dry.

Then I scratched it out.
Too late.
The system had already logged it.

Abuelita didn't even wince.
Just gave me a long, disapproving once-over.

"¿A dónde vas vestido así?"
(Where are you going dressed like that?)

"Voy a ver a Diana. Le voy a dar una sorpresa."
(I'm going to see Diana. I want to surprise her.)

She stared so hard, I swear the room dropped five degrees.

Then, cool as sabotage, she asked:

"¿Antes de irte, puedes ir a la bodega y comprarme flores para
mi Virgencita?"
(Before you go, can you run to the store and buy me flowers for
my Virgin Mary?)

Mic drop.

I laughed. Sharp. Dry.

"No puedo ahora. Te lo hago luego."
(Can't right now. I'll do it later.)

I kissed her cheek and walked.
The door swallowed her final glance.

And just like in her dream,
I left her stranded at sea—
adrift in a story I kept rewriting.

The door clicked shut.

And Abuelita, left alone in the silence,
turned to no one in particular and murmured:

"Como un perro vuelve a su vómito, así el tonto repite su
locura."[68]
(Like a dog returns to its vomit, so the fool repeats his folly.)

---

68 **Como un perro vuelve a su vómito:** From Proverbs 26:11: "As a dog
returns to its vomit, so fools repeat their folly." Abuelita's use of scripture frames
Danne's mistakes as archetypal, not just personal—less scolding than prophecy.
In that moment she emerges as more than caretaker: a keeper of generational
memory and a quiet oracle, her sharp love rooted in spiritual intelligence.

CHAPTER SEVENTEEN

The Vessel & the Flame

Like a lost prophet, I wandered into the bodega stitched into
the ligament of the borough.

Dressed in my finest suit,
red sneakers catching the light,
I stepped into that spectrum-soaked whirlwind
like a man still convinced he could rewrite his night.
Some places don't even feel real until you're standing in them.

A moth to flame.
And the flame was the city—buzzing with danger,
flickering with romance.

Behind the counter, Stanley was mid-marital meltdown.
His voice climbed the shelves like a furious ghost.

Near the lotto machine,
some dude muttered in Spanglish about government cameras
hiding in the coffee cups.

And then—Chico.
He popped out from behind the Goya aisle like a demon
bunny,
grinning with the mischief of something conjured, not born.

"Hey, look at you, Morir Soñado!"
he said, eyebrows dancing.

I navigated the aisles like a general inspecting troops,
trying to avoid him—
but there was no battlefield I could win tonight.

Corner-store flowers—
bright as a Van Gogh hallucination.
Box of gum.
Boom.
Redemption, just barely within reach.

But then—
like lightning on a cloudless day—
the vibe shifted.

I drifted into the pet food aisle,
heart pounding with the thrill of petty crime.

With the stealth of a teenage raccoon,
I planted a can of dog food among the cat tins—
a tiny rebellion against order,
a silent protest against the neat categories I'd been trapped in
all my life.

Pure anarchism.
Perfectly portioned.

The aisle stretched too long,
like a hallway in a dream.
Cans lined up like blank-eyed witnesses, waiting.
And weirdly, the absurdity grounded me.

Behind me, Chico laughed.

Warm.
Familiar.
Almost forgotten.

For a second,
I forgot what I was doing.
Something tugged—
like a thread caught on a nail.
I didn't look down.

Then Chico called my name,
and the moment unraveled.

He shuffled into view,
restocking shelves,
oblivious—
until his vibe changed.

The air didn't just cool;
it recoiled.
Like it knew what was coming.

He looked up.
Dead serious.

"Danne," he said, voice low, "I need to talk to you."

I raised an eyebrow.
"Can't right now. Don't you see how I'm dressed?"
I motioned to the fit—
red sneakers, black suit.
The uniform of a man about to beg forgiveness he probably
didn't deserve.

But Chico didn't shrink.

Didn't budge.

His stare held the softness of a last confession—
like he wasn't just telling me something,
but handing it over carefully, in case it broke.

"It's something special."

"Something special is about to happen to me, Chico."

He shook his head, slow and solemn.
"No, Danne. You won't believe what happened."

I sighed,
curiosity already nipping at my heels.
"All right. Go ahead."

Chico looked around
like we were trading state secrets,
then leaned in and whispered:
"Danne ... someone offered me a thousand dollars for my
Ragnarok character today."

I blazed.
"Incredible! Did you sell?"

His face dropped like a sad balloon.
"I couldn't."

"Why?"

He stared down at his shoes—
worn, loyal, more him than any photo.
"I've grown attached."

And there it was.

Not about the money.[69]
Not even about the game.
It was about identity.
Belonging.
That pixelated version of himself
made more sense than the flesh-and-blood one standing in
front of me.

The joke was there.
Waiting.
An easy out.

But I held it.
Let my face soften.

"Chico," I said, gently exasperated,
"it's a character. That's rent money."

He swallowed.
"But if I sell him ... what am I without him?"

I opened my mouth—gaping.
And then closed it—immediately.

There it was—
the thing beneath the joke.
The wire humming under the laugh.

Because I knew.

---

69 **Not about the money:** Ragnarok is an online role-playing game where
avatars evolve through quests and combat. For Chico, his character is more than
play—it's a digital extension of self. Refusing to sell it underscores how, for
those facing instability or erasure, a virtual self can feel more authentic than the
everyday one. What seems trivial becomes sacred: not money, but memory and
identity.

Give up the one thing holding your shape,
and maybe you disappear.

Not all at once.
Just—
voice,
then face,
then why you ever mattered.

I didn't say it.
Just let the silence do its job.

He was talking about a character.
But he might as well have been talking about me.

I exhaled.
Grounded.
"You're Chico," I said.
"The Boy Wonder."

He lit up like I'd knighted him in aisle three.
"Chico the Boy Wonder," he repeated,
trying it on like a new cape.
"Yeah ... I like that."

He puffed out his chest, then paused.
Voice softened.
Eyes wandered.

"Nah ... I wouldn't trade what makes me, me."
Then, quieter:
"Maybe you're holding onto something too, Danne."

He shifted his weight.
Walked away.

166

And there it was—
my stance,
my tell,
reflected back at me.

Watching myself in a warped mirror—
and not liking what I saw.

His words didn't land loud.
They just hung there.
Quiet.
Hot.
Like something inside me had been moved,
and I wasn't sure I wanted to know what it was.

Then—he tripped over a crate of mangoes.

I sighed
as he shuffled back to his nest—
less built than hoarded.
A sagging pile of habits and hand-me-downs,
stitched together wrong
and forgotten in a corner nobody ever fixed.

It was the kind of place
where things only held together
if you didn't look too hard.

Where everything remained quiet
as long as you played along.

Once you realized
you were part of what kept it stable,
you stopped expecting anything to stay that way on its own.

We all cling to something that makes us feel real—
even if it's just pixels on a screen.
Even if it's the only version of ourselves we know how to love.

But tonight?
I wasn't a vessel anymore.
I was flame,
barely held by fabric.

And I was ready to burn everything—
beautifully.

Chapter Eighteen

Bouquet Bomb

The sun stretched golden fingers across the city,
turning windows into glimmering shards,
washing the streets in an Impressionist haze.

It was the kind of evening where anything felt possible—
where love could be resurrected with the right words,
or at least a half-decent bouquet and a little swagger.

And there I was—strutting.
Sharp suit.
Red sneakers, sabotaging the illusion of a man with his shit
together.
Bouquet in one hand.
Gum in my pocket.
Breath mints masking the stink, not the damage.

My lungs were a church under renovation—
scaffolding where something used to sing.

Destination: the temple of love.
Diana's apartment.

But love's a trickster god.
And I should've known better.

Just as I reached for the buzzer, the building door creaked open
like a stage curtain—
and out stepped a woman dipped in sunset,
hips moving like a saxophone solo.

I held the door.
She passed without a word.

I stared too long.
Beauty makes fools of the faithful.

Her eyes never met mine,
but I swear they stayed on me anyway.

Then I snapped back.
The mission.
Diana.

From behind the door, voices leaked like steam from a cracked
pipe.

"I'm not walking your dog," a young man said.

"You're not walking my dog?" Diana answered—
sharp as broken glass.

"That's what I said."

I froze in the stairwell.
Her voice.
His.

Another man.

I climbed like the air itself might snap. Breath shallow—knife-
thin. My heartbeat wasn't fast. It was furious.

The stairwell stretched like it didn't want me to get there in time. Halfway up, I sprayed mint into my mouth like holy water.

"I'm not doing it."
"What do you mean you're not doing it?"
"The dog's crazy."
"His name is Sydney," Diana snapped. "He's a he."
"He, she, it—I'm not doing it."

He, she, it—who the hell was this guy?

"You owe me," Diana said, voice shifting into that lethal sweet register.
"Remember when you broke up with that chick?
You were crying. Naked. On the couch."

I clenched the railing like it might keep me from unraveling.

The sound of someone being replaced.

"Jesus Christ."
"Jesus Santos," she corrected, with a smile I could hear.

Each word a match dropped into my bloodstream.

I watched from the shadows—half-spy, half-exorcist—
praying the devil I feared wasn't real.

But the longer I listened, the clearer it got:
This man was inside.
Not just the building.
Her.

"What was her name again? Oh yeah—Selena."
"You said her name. That's low."

"Low, but effective."
"Fine. I'll walk your damn dog. But only if you go to the
movies with me next Saturday."
"Can't. Nails."
"Sunday?"
A pause.
A transaction.
"Sunday. But you're walking the dog the whole weekend.
Including Friday night."
"Fine."

And then—to twist the knife—
he kissed her cheek.

That was it.
The trigger.

I stepped out of the shadows.
Storm in my chest.
The bouquet clenched like a pipe bomb of petals.

The flowers had wilted just enough
to look like they regretted being part of this.

He brushed past me.
Unaware of how close he came to eating concrete.

I didn't speak.
I didn't breathe.

I stomped up to Diana's door.
Bouquet clenched like a weapon.

Knock-knock-knock.

"Who is it?"

"Danne."

The door opened.

Diana stood barefoot, calm as moonlight,
and looked me over.
Suit.
Sneakers.
A man trying to dress his wounds in flowers.

"Well, hello there," she said.
"You're looking ... important."

"Why don't you ask me to walk your damn dog?"

Her brow furrowed.

Confusion bloomed.
A twitch at the mouth. A tilt of the head.
Like her face was trying to form a question it didn't trust.

Then—her face softened.
Just a flicker.
Just enough to make my anger hesitate.

And that hesitation?
That made everything worse.

My voice broke the dam.

"You ... YOU ... FUCKING BITCH!"

I shoved the bouquet at her like it could sting.
Then turned and ran.

Down the stairs. Past jazz hips. Out the door.

Into the street, where even the air felt like it was laughing at me.

The taste of mint still lingered—sharp, chemical, almost sacred.

Underneath it:
Dust.
Tomatoes.
Regret.

Behind me, her voice blurred into something muffled:

"DANNE! GET BACK HERE!
That was my cousin Giuseppe, you idiot!"

WHAM!

The bouquet hit the wall.
Petals exploded—fluttering down like confetti at the funeral of my ego.

And somewhere deep inside, something cracked.
Not loud. But final.
Like the first hairline fracture in a mirror that won't stop spreading.

I didn't see my reflection in the glass.
Just a scatter of petals.
A version of myself I didn't recognize.

The crack in me had a name now—and it was hers.

And somewhere, I could hear Chico again:

"Maybe you're holding onto something too, Danne."

I thought I'd dropped it.

But maybe it was still clenched in me.
Blooming.

CHAPTER NINETEEN

The Initiation of the Fool[70]

The streets thrummed, sweating sodium—fevered, restless, alive.
Laughter spilled from alleys and rooftops.
Sirens harmonized with basslines, a symphony of hangovers waiting to happen.
Even the air felt spiked—tequila and unresolved kinetic energy.
A storm, already brewing.

Outside, the nightclub roared—a cathedral of sin where saints wore sequins, and angels smoked clove cigarettes on the roof.
Mischief. Nostalgia.
The scent of unfinished business.
All of it reeled me in.

---

70 **The Initiation of the Fool:** In Jungian psychology, the Fool is the threshold archetype—not naïve so much as unformed: pure potential with a built-in risk of ruin. He steps off the known path under the Trickster's tug, where discovery and self-betrayal blur. Initiation always costs: a skin shed, a name that no longer fits. Whoever crosses doesn't return the same—sometimes, he doesn't return at all.

Leo stood at the entrance like a trickster god,[71] leaning against
the doorframe with that signature smirk—
the kind that can rewrite or ruin destinies.

"There he is. Took you long enough," he grinned.
"I knew you'd show."

"Yeah? How?"

He sniffed the air, all dramatic.
"You're my blood. I can smell when you're in trouble."

He wasn't wrong.

He saw it in my face: I wasn't just hurting;
I was unmoored.

I didn't come to forget Diana.
I came to remember who I was before her.
And maybe kill that version of me too.

Leo slung an arm over my shoulder.
The second we stepped inside, the music consumed us whole.

▼

From the other side of town, behind the Honey Buns, Chico
peeked out—
eyes wide like he was watching a telenovela his abuela swore

---

71 **Trickster god:** Leo echoes the archetypal trickster—Loki, Anansi, Coyote—
agents of chaos who provoke change through temptation and misdirection. He
doesn't heal but detours, masking instability with charisma. As gatekeeper to
Danne's initiation, he offers pleasure dressed as destiny, revelation blurred with
sabotage.

was too spicy for his age.

Stanley was getting cooked.
Phone in hand, forehead gleaming—like he was in round
twelve of a breakup bout.
No gloves. No coach. No bell to save him.

"Mi amor," he crooned, syrup-thick and shaking, "how you
gon' say that to me? I'm out here grindin' for you and the
girls."

The lights buzzed above like even they didn't want to get
involved.
One hand held the phone.
The other swatted at the air like the smoke was real.

"You know I gotta be cariñoso (affectionate) to my customers,"
Stanley pleaded, voice cracking on the word like it had cyanide
laced in the vowels.
"It's part of the hustle, baby, come on—"

But cariñoso?
That was the killshot.
The word cracked like a bone in a silence too loud to ignore.

Chico didn't hear what came next.
Didn't need to.
He just felt it—
like betrayal got a bullhorn
and pointed it straight at Stanley's soul.

Time lost grip.

179

Lights flickered like dying stars.
Bodies moved like puppets pulled by invisible threads.

And then—a laugh.
Not Diana's, but close.
Too close.
High, with that same wicked curl that used to nest behind my ear.

My gut yanked sideways—
toward the sound.
Toward her memory.

But it vanished.
Folded back into the music.
Or maybe the unraveling had already begun.

Leo led me to the back room.
The walls breathed.
The shadows whispered.

Psychedelic purgatory—
bathed in red and violet, like limbo got a makeover from a
demigod with a glue gun and a god complex.

He poured two drinks.
Liquid fire that shimmered in colors I didn't have names for.

"To baby mamas who don't ask questions,
and side chicks who know their role."

I hesitated.
"Leo ... what if you saw your girl kiss another guy?"

He didn't hesitate.

"I'd dump da bitch and get a new one."

Efficient. Inhuman.
Like he'd never been tethered to anything.
Never stayed long enough to bruise.

"Nah," I said. "I don't want anybody else. I want her."

Leo laughed—not like a man,
but like something with wings.

Then came the vessel.
Glass. Small.
The liquid inside pulsed like it had a heartbeat.
Like it was watching.

Leo poured it into my glass.
The liquid hit like it had weight—thick, sludgy, the color of
mud.
It didn't pour. It dragged itself.

"Taste this bad boy."
"What is it?"
"Just drink it."
"That's what they said at Jonestown."[72]
"Jesus. Drink the damn thing."

And because the night had teeth,
and Leo had charm,
and I had nothing left to lose—
I drank.

---

72 **Jonestown:** Danne's quip recalls the 1978 mass suicide where followers of
Jim Jones drank poisoned Kool-Aid.

Bitter as bark boiled in regret.
Thick as fermented grief.
Mud soaked in metal.
Over-steeped tea left to rot.
Finished with burnt coffee taste,
and a plant's holy revelation.

It doesn't go down easy because it's not done speaking.
And somehow, buried beneath the bile?
Truth. Sharp. Sour. Sacred.

But beneath even that—
a spark.

"That shit's disgusting," I coughed.

Leo cackled. "You'll feel better by morning."

But the night disagreed.

The room twisted.
The music coiled around me—serpentine, knowing.

"You think she did it to make me jealous?"
"Jesus Christ," Leo groaned. "Let it go. What you need—"
He clapped my shoulder. "Is someone new."

"Leo, I just broke up with my girlfriend."

"Trust me."
Grinning.
"You'll forget all about that ho."

He adjusted my collar like he was prepping me for execution.
"Don't move. I'll be right back."

Alone, I sank into the couch.

The bass became heartbeats.
The walls pulsed.
Something traced the back of my neck—breath that didn't belong.

Diana's name still whispered in my bloodstream—
a protection spell too weak to hold against this.

Then the door opened.

Leo returned—
strobe-lit, victorious.

And she followed.

She didn't walk.
She arrived.

Porcelain. Electric.
An illusion coded in after-glow and perfume.

Leo beamed. "Danne, this is Eva.
What'd I tell you? Knockout, right?"

"Cute," I said.

"Cute?" Leo barked. "She's a goddess."

When Eva turned,
her eyes weren't just almond-shaped.
They were ageless.

"Nice to meet you," I managed.

"I'm sure it is," she purred.

Leo clapped, triumphant.
"Make yourselves comfortable."

I didn't move.
The warmth in my chest bloomed.
"Leo ..." I croaked. "What was in that drink?"

"By the time it kicks in," he grinned,
"you won't even recognize yourself."

The club pulsed around us.
Everything throbbed—walls, floor, bassline. But the beat felt a
half-second out of sync with the music.

Eva and I floated. Weightless.
The moment stretched too long,
like time was watching, not passing.
She swirled her glass like it held secrets—
and not once did the ice clink.

"Correct me if I'm wrong," I said, voice syrup-thick,
"but I swear I've met you before."

Her eyes didn't reflect the lights.
They gobbled them—like they were hungry for it.

"Probably," she said. Like the word meant nothing.

She looked at me like people look at old photos—nostalgic, but
with no memory of taking them.

"What about you?" she asked.
"Looks like you're doing alright."

"I wish."
I rubbed my face, like I could wipe the shame off.

"Got played. Shit hurts."

She didn't gleam the whole time I spoke. Not once.
I only noticed when she finally did—slow, mechanical, like it
was for my sake.

She rolled her eyes.

"People stay fake. Always got a mask on. But this?"
She motioned to the velvet-glow swirl of the room.
"This is real. You and me. Just vibes."

It did feel good. That was the problem.

There was a current between us—
not seen, not touched, but felt.
Like the air changed pressure, everything leaning toward her.

She looked at me like she already knew.
Like this was inevitable.
Like I'd been walking toward her from the second I saw her.

I didn't decide to lean in.
I just did.
Like my body was answering a question
my mind hadn't formed yet.

Our mouths met.
Quick. Electric.
But it didn't feel innocent; it felt preordained.

Heat moved between us—not warmth, but something more
focused.
Sharpened.
It pressed through the air,

through the sliver of space still left between our bodies.

And whatever was asleep in me began to stir. Like I'd been chosen—not seduced.

She didn't speak.
Just pressed her hand to my chest—cooler than skin should be, like she'd been holding something frozen.

Her thigh brushed mine—deliberate, but too smooth, like muscle trained to mimic feeling.

She leaned in, breath grazing my ear—
not a whisper, not a moan, just that sound people make when they forget they're being heard.

A pull—low and electric—like my body remembered something my mind hadn't caught up to.
Like I'd been circling a signal I didn't know belonged to her.

Then—clarity.
Sharp. Sudden.
One dying neuron firing its last flare.

I froze.
She mirrored.

"Relax, Papi ..."
Then, closer:
"What's wrong? You don't like girls?"

I laughed—dry.
"Of course I do. It's just—"

My brain split like glass under heat—one voice whispering what's the harm, the other screaming get out.

Before I could answer,
she whispered again:
"Don't you wanna kick it?"

She lingered in the space between question and command.
Her eyes went obsidian—bottomless, like looking down a well
and seeing no reflection.

"What—I'm not pretty enough for you?"

"Eva ..."
Careful.

Like I was defusing a bomb with my breath.
"You're beautiful. No lie.
But maybe ... some other lifetime."

She laughed.
Not for me.
Not human.
Just hollow.

"Now look who's the fake one."

Then she turned.
Walked away.
"Miss me."

Vanished into the crowd
like a thought you regret the second it's gone.

And somehow—
the space she left behind felt heavier.
Something was still sitting across from me. Watching—like it
had never left. Not her, but the thing behind her eyes.

▼

The whole bodega held its breath.
Even the fridge full of Arizona cans froze—like it knew not to interrupt.

Chico didn't move.
Couldn't.

The air was thick, buzzing like a bug zapper mid-summer.
And just like that—something shifted.

Stanley snapped.

"¿Qué, qué, quién te dijo eso?"
(What, what, who said that to you?)

His voice ricocheted off the linoleum like a bottle breaking in a stairwell—sharp, echoing, way too loud for a man trying to hold on.

"You can't be listenin' to people like that. People be hatin'. They don't got shit else to do but run they mouth."

Uh-oh.

Chico's eyes went wide.
Stanley was cussin' now.
Line crossed.
Point of no return.
The air felt thick, like a storm was brewing in the pit of his stomach. Just like last time.

"They just mad 'cause me and you solid, baby!
You know that.

Everybody know that!"

Stanley started pacing.
Frantic.
Mop of dignity dragging behind him
like he was auditioning for a one-man tragedy.
He'd sworn he'd never let anyone shake him this way again.
Not after last time.

Then—*boom.*
That pause.
The kind of pause that don't just kill a conversation
but puts it in a casket.
Stanley could feel the weight of it,
like the air itself was holding him down,
making him stand still when every part of him wanted to flee.

Even Chico felt it.
That moment when the universe flips a coin.
And you already know it's landing wrong side up.

"¿Ah, tú le vas a creer a ella más que a mí?"
(Oh, you're going to believe her more than me?)
His voice cracked—not from weakness, but from knowing this
was it.
The last card.
All in.
There was no turning back now. Whatever was left of them,
whatever trust had held them together, was slipping away with
each word.

Stanley's breath hitched.
Everything in him screamed to stop, to take it back—

but it was already too late.

"¿Ah, sí? Entonces, ¿por qué no te vas al diablo?"
(Oh, really? Then why don't you go to hell?)

Click.
Phone hit the counter like a judge sentenced someone to life.

Silence.
The kind that hums.

Stanley stood there.
Just breathing.
Like he'd run full speed into the past and lost.

Then something snagged his eye: a can of dog food jammed
among the cat tins. A slip-up—or maybe a sign.
"Chico!" he called, the word flaring sharp as a match-strike.
"Yeah, Stanley?"

▼

Back at the club.
Leo found me fast—like he'd been waiting.
"What the hell happened?"
He looked around, eyes piercing.
"What did you say to her?"
Like I had lit a match in a gas station.

I didn't answer.
Everything felt off.
Tilted.

"Leo ... I feel weird."

Pause.
"Like really weird."

He squinted.
"Did you get any?"

"Nah."
I shook my head.
"She was nice, but something was off, man.
Like some déjà vu shit."[73]

Leo took a moment to let it sink in.
"What the hell's that—déjà vu?"

Every word she spoke felt familiar, but wrong—
like reading a diary you don't remember writing.
It wasn't creepy. Just … off.
Like something important was supposed to happen.
And then didn't.

It felt like I'd just lost a winning lottery ticket.

He shook his head, half-laughing.
"Who turns down free stuff? What's wrong—
you don't like girls now?"

I looked at him.
Not with anger. Not even judgment.
Just the slow ache of realizing someone you love stopped
evolving.

----

73 **Déjà vu:** French for "already seen," it names the uncanny sense that a
moment has happened before. Psychologists call it a memory glitch—perception
briefly misfiled as recollection. In literature it's a portal; in trauma, a body's
warning—a nudge to pay attention.

I couldn't help it—had to say the one thing that cut clean.

"Hey, Leo ... don't tell people we're related," I said.
Pause.
"You've never had scruples."

That hit.
Quieter than I expected.
But deeper.

Something flickered behind his eyes—then shut.

"What the fuck is a scruple?" he muttered, like he couldn't afford to understand.

Then under his breath: "Sounds like a pasta."

I almost laughed. Almost.
Then I left.

That was Leo.

Oh, Uncle Leo.
I never told anyone we were blood.
If asked, I always said he was a distant cousin.
Part cover story.
Part demolition crew.

He'd yank temptation from my grip,
speak of discipline with chaos in his eyes,
then hand me a lesson I never asked to learn.

And when shit hit the fan—
he was the fan.

This wasn't betrayal.

It was grief.

Like I wrote him in to save the scene,
gave him the hero's lines—
and he ad-libbed the villain.

▼

Outside, the city quivered.
Not just alive, but hunting.
Not like a rush.
Like a rewind.
Like peeling back the world's wallpaper
and touching something that wasn't meant to be felt.

New York:
a beast with too many eyes
and no eyelids.

The sidewalks warped.
Every face looked
almost familiar.

Like a dream
I forgot to wake up from.

Then—the drug hit.

I could feel the streets coursing through my spine.

And suddenly, I was nine
staring at da Vinci's Vitruvian Man.

Four arms.
Four legs.

Flesh pinned to symmetry.
A prototype God forgot to finish.
With his Johnson hanging out.

I stepped into whatever this was.
Walked like it had already been written.
Like I'd been baptized in fire.

A heat lamp buzzed above a couple at the outdoor tables—
blue-lit, blank-faced,
eyes chained to their screens,
plates untouched,
like they were full of notifications.

Steam curling.
Not vapor.
Something leaving them.

They didn't even notice me
until I was right there.

No intro. No excuse.
I just lifted my arms—
and they stood—like they'd been waiting for the signal.

Eyes glazed.
Limbs slow.
I pulled them into a hug.

At first, they were slack.
Then—they held me back.

Not out of love.
Out of respect.

And then—they kissed.

Not sweet.
Not sexy.
An exorcism.

Like two phonographs finding the same song after years of
static.

That kiss healed something—
not between them,
but in me.

I stepped back.
Lifted my arms to the sky
like I'd just nailed the impossible.

I walked. Or floated. Until I saw him.

Curled on concrete.
Not just homeless.
Primeval.
Like he'd climbed out of my ribcage
when I wasn't looking.

I reached into my pocket.
A crumpled bill.
Like it had been waiting.

He took it.
Shaking.
Mumbled something.

A prayer. A curse.
My name. In a dead language.

I ran.

▼

The subway didn't swallow me.
It remembered me.

I puked. Not food—something older.
The bile came with heat and hiss,
like tapeworms of memory
detaching from the lining of my soul.
It slithered up through spine and throat—
thick, hot, ancestral.

My body folded in half,
knees kissing dirt like it was scripture.
And still—more came.

It wasn't just vomiting. It was extraction.

Each heave was a crowbar, prying shame from the marrow.
Regret. Rage.
The names of people I never forgave—especially myself.
They came out in chunks,
like curses I'd swallowed years ago and never digested.

I shook—
but not from illness.
From surrender.
Like something inside me had been chained to a furnace
and the link just snapped.

My mouth foamed prayers I didn't recognize,
in a language that sounded older than words.

Ribs aching—
like I was giving birth to the part of me I buried to survive.

This wasn't purging.
It was a reckoning—
penance pulled through flesh,
judgment by bile.

When it was done,
I wasn't empty.
I was clean—
in the way a battlefield is clean once the fire has passed.

My hands reached for the bench
like they were searching for my name.

The world didn't shimmer.
It exhaled.

And for the first time in years,
so did I.

The train arrived—chrome wrapped in prophecy.
Its howl sang in bone-language.
Doors opened like a dare.

I wiped my mouth, steadied my breath,
and let the train take me.

I stepped in.

The floor pulsed.
Faces bent and blinked—too long, too knowing.

The ceiling whispered my name like it remembered me from
somewhere deeper.

I didn't sit.
I floated.

The train lurched forward—
not through the city,
but through some memory the future forgot to have.

I wiped my mouth, straightened my jacket,
and stepped onto the train.

The moment the doors hissed shut,
the weight changed.
Heavy.

Something unseen leaned close—too close—
like it wanted to try my name on its tongue.

I slumped into the seat.
My head hit the window
and melted into every person
that rode this line before me.

A breath.

Then I saw it.
My reflection.
But not me.

The version of me
who thought love was something to win,
not something to survive.

His head slanted—wrong.
Lagging.

Then—his lips moved.

One word.
Silent.

And I felt it crack me.
Not heartbreak.
Something deeper.
A rupture.[74]

Like a fault line.
Finally giving way.

The train lurched. My reflection didn't.

I turned fast. He followed late.

I raised my hand. He mirrored—too slow.

His lips moved again. Not mine. His.

No sound. Just shape.
A secret I already knew.

I leaned in.
Whispered: "What?"

He grinned. Wider than me.

Then—gone.

Just me again—almost.

The train screeched into Dyckman.
I stumbled out. The doors slammed.

---

74 **The rupture on the train:** A glitched "mirror moment" where Danne glimpses his shadow self—hidden, denied, emerging. The reflection lags, the smile too wide, the lips moving without sound. Is he splitting, seeing who he'll become or what he's lost?

And behind them, he stayed.
Still grinning.

It was me.
But wrong.
Crooked—off just enough to feel dangerous.

And I didn't know
if I'd left him behind ...
or if he was the one walking forward now.

▼

The world collapsed.
Then I fell.
Through the glass mirror.
Into something deeper.

A couch.
Eva.
But not.

She flickered—girl, woman, dream, ghost.

Her voice was everywhere—sweet as cherries,
hot as a cauldron's kiss.

"I'm here because you opened the door."

My hands—slick.

Red.
Not blood.
Just the debt of choosing wrong.

"You felt it. The itch.
The voice you ignore.
One more night.
One more mouth."

She leaned in.

"I'm not a girl.
I'm the mirror."

I didn't argue.
What could I say
to a truth like that?

I couldn't speak.

"What's wrong?
Not pretty enough for you?"

Her voice split—
two mouths.
One truth.

"Now look who's the fake one."

Then—
Diana.
Crying.
Everywhere.

The room cracked.
The walls exhaled.
Eva vanished.
But her voice stayed:
"Pretend I was never real. But I'll be waiting."

She touched my chest.
The lights surrendered.
One last breath.
Then—total black.

Then—light.
Room. Cold air.

I woke up.
But not all of me came back.

My chest burned. My hands shook.
No mark. But she was still there. Watching.

Next thing I knew, I was on the bench at the station—
folded like laundry still warm from the flames.

My body didn't even feel like mine.
Like my skin showed up
but left my soul behind at the last stop.

That weight in my chest?
Not grief.
Not guilt.
Just the crack where the mirror used to be.

I closed my eyes. And passed out.

In the distance, a dog barked.

Sydney.
Still waiting to be walked.

CHAPTER TWENTY

Made in China

The city had the stale breath of early morning—
wet pavement, burnt coffee, piss simmering in alleyways.
But the sun, soft and stupid with hope, still kissed the rooftops
like nothing had ever gone wrong.

I stepped into the light like something newly hatched,
flashing against it, limbs dragging,
still tangled in the hallucinations of the night before.

Hudson Pier was the only tether I had to anything real.
And sometimes, you don't know you're looking for grace
until your feet are already moving.

I didn't know where else to go.

I turned west, chasing silence—
pretending the Hudson could rinse the night out of my
bloodstream.

Left foot. Right foot. Left foot. Right foot.
Each one dragging guilt like a broken promise,
bones rehearsing a crime the mind tried to forget.
And with every step:
you're still here.

The guardrail was cold beneath my palm—
something solid while everything else stuttered like busted
gears.

I stared at the river.
The ripples moved like memory—half-formed, half-denied.
That subway reflection still clung to my skull,
refusing to line up with the man I thought I was.

Then—Chico.
His hand—shaking—tore through the hallucination like a
blade through canvas.
Reality rushed in like a lungful of ice.

"Chico, what the f—?"
He was panting, wild-eyed, smeared with something red and
raw.
"Danne," he rasped, "I need to tell you something."

I barked out a laugh. Dry.
"And here I thought I had a rough night."

He didn't laugh.
"Last night, I … I …"
"What?" I asked, grabbing at humor like a drowning man.
"You sold your Ragnarok character?"

His hands twitched.
"Danne. I need you to listen to me."
And that broke through.
Something in his voice cracked against my firewall.

"Alright," I said, softer.
"I'm listening."

"Stanley got into a fight with his wife—on the phone—"

I never heard the rest.
The air tilted—quietly, just enough to feel it.
That quiet charge before everything tips.

"Wait," I interrupted.
"What time is it?"

"Eight o'clock."

"Unbelievable."

And just like that—Mikey and Moreno stepped out of the fog.
Two ghosts with fists.
One ritual short of a sacrifice.

"I thought you pussies weren't gonna show," Mikey grinned.

"And miss watching you get smoked? Never," I shot back.

"You bring the gloves?"

"Got 'em right here," Moreno said, tossing a pair like a magician.

"You don't have to do this," I whispered to Chico. "Your call."

Mikey cracked his knuckles.

"So what's the play?"

The air went still.
Boys shuffled like chess pieces—
ceremony snapping into place.

"Three rounds. Queensberry rules,"[75] I said.
Setting limits. Hoping they'd hold.

"That's it?" Mikey scoffed.

"That's all my man needs."

I turned to Chico. Anchored him.

Chico's hands trembled as I tightened the laces.

"Keep your head down.
Move.
Don't plant unless you're throwing."

"Think I got a shot?"

"If you keep moving, let the clock run—you might walk out of
this alive."

Moreno whispered poison in Mikey's ear.

"Fuck'em up."

"Danne—"

"Later. Stay with me."

He nodded.

And the whistle snapped the world into motion.

Round one.

---

75 **Queensberry rules:** Evokes the illusion of control. *Queensberry rules* refer
to 19th-century boxing regulations—invoked here ironically. Danne uses them
as a coping mechanism, a way to impose order on something unraveling. It's
ritualized violence dressed as structure, meant to contain chaos—but it doesn't.

They touched gloves—
a pact with an expiration date.

Then circled.
Revolved.
Two moons with no center of gravity.

Mikey struck first.
A right.
Chico dodged, barely, and lunged—grabbing hold like
something in him still wanted to live.

Then—
Mikey slammed him down. Into the ground.

Hard.
But Chico rose.
Bleeding.
Breathing.

A jab—red bloomed on his cheek.

"Has your boy had enough?" Moreno called.

"He's just getting started."

Chico spat. Wiped his mouth.

Then—a wild haymaker.
And it landed.

Mikey hesitated. Staggered.

Then his face changed.

Uppercut.

Time snapped.
Chico left the ground.
The world folded.

He crashed.

A sound followed—wet, final.

Then—not silence.
Absence.

Moreno tore off Chico's gloves.
Mikey stood there, hollowed out, waiting for the tape to rewind.

Then they disappeared into the fog.

I was already moving.

"Chico—c'mon, man."

Too limp.
Too quiet.

This wasn't just Chico on the ground.
It was every version of me that couldn't save the people I loved.

"Chico."

Nothing.

▲

Then—a sparkle.
Somewhere inside him,
a dream rebooted.

He wasn't here anymore.
Not fully.

Rachel.
Not real—just the echo he needed.
A memory shaped soft and forgiving,
stitched from midnight, shame, and want.

She leaned in.
Traced his chest like she was drawing a map
back to who he used to be.
She kissed him.

Time held its breath.
No wind. No weight. Just hush.

Then—*snap.*

Rachel gone.
Dream gone.
River back.
Sky bruised.
And I couldn't move—just waited
for him to come to his senses.

▼

"Chico, wake up."

A flutter.
A groan.

"What ... happened?"

"You got knocked out."

"I'm sorry, Danne. I fell ..."
Like he was still arguing with ghosts.

He fumbled in his pocket.
Pulled out a rosary.
Pressed it into my hand like a secret.

Plastic beads.
Crucifix.

Weightless.
Brutal.

"Made in China."

It almost made me laugh.

Then—he bolted.

"Chico!"

I chased him down the slope. The street blurred as I ran.
"Stop!"
But the headlights were already cutting through the dusk—
fast, low, locked on the curve.

Chico slipped and tried to catch himself—
but it was too late.

The car slammed up against his torso.
The sound—metal, bone, final.

His body twisted and his right leg curled beneath him.
Blood spread—slow at first, then faster.

The park froze like a blizzard in mid-January.

I dropped beside him. Didn't know if touching would help—
but I couldn't not.

His blood was on me before I even touched him.

"Breathe. Chico. Stay with me."

His eyes locked on mine.

"Danne ... I didn't mean to ..."

"I know," I said but I didn't. "Tell me the book you're reading
now?"

A flutter. Slow.

"Kavalier & Clay ..."[76]

And then—stillness.

The city kept moving, but Chico didn't.

I placed the rosary back in his hand.
But his fingers wouldn't close.

His hand stayed open.
Like a question mark the city never answered.

I saved Petey, but I couldn't save Chico—
and I still don't know which one I dream about more.

Maybe it's because part of me still believes there was something

---

76 *Kavalier & Clay*: Michael Chabon's novel follows two Jewish comic
creators who turn trauma into myth through their hero, *The Escapist*. Chico
relates: he builds masks too—through humor, trivia, avatars. Like Chabon's duo,
fiction is his armor. This links him to Danne: one masked in sarcasm, the other
in smarts. Different fronts, same fight. The mask isn't a lie; it's a lifeline.

I missed.
Some angle.
Some second.
Some version of the night where I move faster, think smarter,
do more.

And what haunts me most is knowing there wasn't a redo. And
something locked in me. Hard and permanent.

Like a door that would never open again.

Eventually, a cop tapped me on the shoulder,
 and my words trickled out as if the world was undersea.

"No ... I don't have a gun."

CHAPTER TWENTY-ONE

The Pitcher in the Rye[77]

The afternoon sun knifed through Inwood, splitting the last scraps of shadow. Broken glass near the curb caught fire—tiny embers of ruin.

Dr. Coen shuffled through it, hunched, a grocery bag of oranges clutched to his chest. They pressed into him like puppies. In his other hand: a cigarette. The kind of contradiction that almost deserved applause.

He fumbled with a match.
The flame hiccupped.
His shoulders twitched—the reflex of someone being watched.

He turned.
Scanned the street.
But the city just stared back—vague, indifferent, chewing gum, looking the other way.

Then he turned the corner.

------

77 **The Pitcher in the Rye:** A play on *The Catcher in the Rye*, but flipped— from protector to aggressor. In Salinger's novel, Holden Caulfield envisions himself saving children from falling into adulthood, corruption, or despair but here Danne is not catching but pitching, and he becomes the fall.

And there I was.

A brick wall in sneakers. Arms crossed.
Bugs Bunny to his Elmer Fudd.

"Need a light, Doc?"

My voice sliced the silence—like a memory that showed up
early.

He flinched.
The bag wobbled.
His face twisted—like he'd bitten something bitter.

"Danne," he said. "What are you doing here?"

I let it sit.

"I'm in trouble."

He straightened.
Click. His professional mask locked into place.

"We can talk tomorrow ... in my office."

"Talk," I echoed, like the word was a flavor I didn't trust.

I nodded at his cigarette.

"Look at you—smoking. After all that dream-state talk—lower
curve, upper curve, OM?
Bullshit. You're just as breakable as the rest of us."

I stepped closer.

"So tell me, Doc—where's the dot now?"

He flinched. Barely.

But I saw it.
Enough.

"I can see you're upset—"

"There it is," I snapped. "Deflection. Classic."

Step. Step.
His heel tapped the wall.
Checkmate.

His mask cracked. Just for a second.
I could've stopped.
But I didn't.

I started circling. Not fast.
Just close enough to make the air tighten.

"I'm sorry you feel that way, Danne."

I slapped the cigarette away.
It spun out—gone.

"You should be," I said.
"You really let me down."

One swipe.
The bag ripped—cans, fruit, shrapnel. An orange rolled into
the street like it had somewhere better to be.

Coen's eyes followed it—like it meant something.

"Danne," he said. "You're scaring me."

But I wasn't listening.
I bent down. Picked up two oranges.
Weighed them like grenades.

"Hey, Doc. I got a title for my book—*The Pitcher in the Rye*."

I hurled the first.
It smacked the wall near his head.

"Get it?" I said. "*The Pitcher in the Rye!*"

The second came harder.
He threw up his palms.

"Is this a prank, Danne? Are you filming me?"

I laughed.
Sharp. Crooked.

Then stepped in.

I wanted to hit him with more than fruit.
I wanted to hit him with every word I never said to Chico.

"You ever notice nobody teaches us how to die?
Twelve years of school and nobody says:
'Hey—one day, you're gonna stop breathing.'
They hand you the Pythagorean theorem but skip grief.
Skip endings.
Skip the kind of loss that marks you forever."

Step closer.

"And you? You hide behind that calm voice, those soft
cardigans—like if you look at death too long, it'll follow you
home."

He knew. I saw it in his eyes.

"Why do grown-ups—people with wills and Hulu murder
docs—pretend death's a rumor?

It's not a pop quiz.
It's the final exam.
And everyone's flunking it by pretending it's not coming."

My voice cracked. But I didn't stop.

"Me? I got the spoiler.
Front row.
Watched my boy fold like a paper crane on Dyckman.
He said my name—and died holding my hand."

Silence. Then the final cut.

"And you wanna give me breathing techniques?"

It all unraveled. Fast.

"Go ahead. Write that down. Ask about my mother.
Ask how it makes me feel.
What's next—a healing worksheet? Circle your trauma, color-code the grief, and act like pain comes with instructions?"

His eyes didn't fight back.
Just stayed wide. Human.

And something in me broke.

I hugged him.
Quick. Fierce.
Final.

When I pulled away, I handed him his key.

"Here," I said.

And I walked.
Left him there—among the spilled groceries and the pieces of

who we were supposed to be.

"Where are you going?" he called.
"Danne, wait. What are you going to do?"

I didn't answer.
His voice hit the air and dropped—like a match struck
underwater.

Across the street, a woman in her fifties clicked to a stop.
Lipstick drawn with military precision.
Hair like a courtroom wig.

"I saw the whole thing—from my window," she said.
"If you want to press charges, I'll testify. Got partial footage.
Some of it's blurry—I was microwaving soup."

Coen blushed.

"That was emotional abuse and physical aggression," she
added, handing him a sticky note with her name and
apartment number.

Then she turned—marched off—like she'd just saved
democracy and still had time to finish her soup.

Coen stood alone.
Groceries scattered. Phone dangling from his hand.
No answers.
Just witnesses.
And a system that always shows up too late.

EPILOGUE

The river sat still. So did we.
Annie stood beside me—hands in her pockets, hood up—like
she'd always been there.
Same pier. Same dark.
Same silence stretching between us, waiting to be broken.

I ran my thumb along my arm—the spot where the dragon
would go. Where it had always belonged. Where I used to
picture ink.

But now, even that felt thin.
Like armor I didn't need anymore.

The tattoo—my myth, my metaphor—felt like something I'd
rehearsed for the wrong audience.
Maybe it was never about rebellion. Not fire or flight.
Maybe it was about Abuelita.

She never got a dragon tattoo. She didn't need one.
She was the dragon—coiled in silence, bound by ritual,
burning behind her rosaries.

I used to think I was the one carrying the fire.
But it was her all along.
She prayed through pain—not out of habit, but instinct.
Like she knew some stories only move forward through loss.

The sun bled out, spilling amber across the skyline.
Up ahead, the George Washington Bridge arched over us—
steel ribs reaching into the sky.
Like the city was trying to cough up a confession.

A jogger passed, earbuds in. Annie didn't flinch.
And that's when I knew:
I didn't need to say it out loud.
Not to her.

The tattoo? It wasn't rebellion.
It was remembrance.

And maybe I didn't need to ink it. Because it was already
there—hidden in my blood, curled behind my ribs, waiting
to be remembered.

The bridge cables looked like veins—tense, twitching.
And against its frame, I unraveled mine. Not like a
confession.
More like a file transfer.

Something I'd carried so long, I couldn't tell where it ended
and I began.

And for a second—I felt Chico.
Watching from the corner.
Smirking through a bruise.
"Maybe you're holding onto something too, Danne."

I didn't say his name. But he was there.

Annie listened. Head tilted. Not reacting to what I said, but
to how I said it—like she was hearing something beneath the
words.

"That's it?" she asked.
Her voice—a lit match in the cooling air.

I shook my head. "No... I left out one detail."

And the silence after that? It did what silence does—made room for truth.

Then time didn't just slip.
It folded in on itself.

Because once you sip memory—real memory, raw honesty—there's no un-drinking it.

We rewound.

▼

I blinked—and the past pulled tight. Not just memory.
Muscle.
Smell.
Blood.
We were back there.

The aisle. The can. The crack.

Stanley stalked the aisles—shoes whispering across linoleum, mood flickering like that cheap lighter he kept snapping open and shut.

Then something snagged his eye: a can of dog food jammed among the cat tins. A slip-up—or maybe a sign.

"Chico!" he called, the word flaring sharp as a match-strike.

"Yeah, Stanley?"

A voice from the dark—thin, brittle, like it had already been loaded in the chamber.

Stanley moved in. Can in hand. Fire in his belly. Projecting all his marital purgatory onto one misplaced label.

"What's this doing in the cat section?"

"I don't know."

"You don't know?"

Then it turned.

Chico didn't flinch. He redirected.

"Stanley... what if you're the one who made the mistake?"

KABOOM.

Stanley fried—red-faced, revival preacher spitting gasoline sermons.

Then the cans started flying—like it was a food drive for the damned.

And then—it happened.

Chico stepped back. A can sliced the air and struck him clean on the crown.

A sickening *thunk.*
He staggered.
Blood welled fast from the split—ran down his forehead, over his brow, his cheek, dripping off his chin.

Everything stopped.
Then—*click.*

The shift.

Eyes rolled. Breath stuttered. No words. No shout.
Just—stillness.
Like something inside flipped off.

Then—without warning—he ducked behind the counter,
ripped the gun from its hiding spot.

Turned—fast, coiled—rage twisting through him like smoke
chasing oxygen.

The space warped. Stanley's hands flew up—like his body
remembered something his mouth didn't.

"Chico, wait—"

But Chico was gone. Not in anger. In ritual. A version of
himself I helped write—now moving on instinct.

"How does this make you feel?" I heard myself ask. Not for
Stanley. For Chico.

Stanley ran—flailing limbs, backpedaled ego.

But Chico? Moved like fate had set a timer. His foot caught a
can. Slipped. Gun fired.

No aim. No warning. Just—*flash.*
Smoke curled in the air—sharp, bitter.

And fate? It answered.

Abuelita. Solid as myth. Old blood. Sharp prayers.
She stepped forward—right into the line of fire.

The bullet caught her in the shoulder.

No scream—just a gasp, a stumble,
fabric folding as her knees buckled.

Her mouth opened—maybe to bless, maybe to curse—but the words never came.

Chico dropped beside her—not to mourn. Not to save. To take.

He unclasped the rosary from her wrist—beads still cool, faintly warmed by her skin.

Then he turned and clipped a can. It spun once, slid across the tile—a soft scrape—and landed in her open hand.

▲

Annie leaned in and scanned me like a barcode.

"Well," she said, "looks like everyone got what they deserve."

"Damn," I said. "You make karma sound like a spreadsheet."

"What about your grandmother?" she asked, eyes tracing me for fallout.

"Abuelita? Are you kidding me, she'll outlive us all," I told her. "She's like a roach—built for the apocalypse."

The joke didn't travel, but she didn't press—like she knew some stories only survive in silence.

"That's what I like about you," I said, "you know how to keep a secret."

"Aww."

"No, I mean it. You're real."

She smirked. "You coming on to me?"

"Nah. Most people talk like they're selling something. You don't. You just show up and listen."

She paused. Then: "You still gonna get that dragon tattoo?"

"Maybe it was never about the tattoo."

"Damn," she said. "That almost sounded smart."

She smiled, but it didn't stick. Like something in her had already moved on. Like she'd heard what she needed.

Maybe I always knew. But knowing and saying aren't the same thing.

I looked over. Annie was still there. Still listening.
But her eyes had that faraway gleam—like she was already filing this under "done."

And for a second, I swear I heard Chico laugh—soft, like wind slipping through a busted vent.

Annie didn't speak. Just leaned in—slow, sure. Like she was sealing something sacred between us.

Her lips found mine—warm, deliberate. The kind of promise people only make with their whole body.

It was soft. Short. But it stayed.

Still—when she pulled back, her eyes didn't linger. Like the moment had passed through her, not into her.

Then—just when I thought I'd slipped out clean—Diana

appeared.
No sound.
No warning.
Just weight.

Annie didn't move. Neither did I. She clocked Diana, gave a single nod.

"Good luck with that," she said.
Then Annie stepped back—like she'd already shelved the story.

No flinch. No goodbye. Just gone.

"And you thought this was over?" Diana said. "It's only getting started."

"For the record," I called, "I AM SPOCK."

Then I ran too. Because sometimes logic means knowing when to bail.

The dark knew we were coming. It made room.

And I realized something strange: Maybe I'll never get that dragon tattoo. Maybe it was never meant to be.

Because scars? They don't ask for permission. They just show up—uninvited and permanent as hell.